HIDDEN MENAGERIE:

A Cryptid Anthology

Vol 1

HIDDEN MENAGERIE:

A Cryptid Anthology

Vol 1

Edited by Michael Cieslak

The
Dragon's Roost Press
2018

Table of Contents

In Search Of...

Cryptozoology: the study of and search for animals and especially legendary animals (such as Sasquatch) usually in order to evaluate the possibility of their existence.

If you were a child in the 1970s and 80s, as I was, you grew up in a world of monsters. There were creature features on late night TV, local shows on the weekends showing everything from Universal classics to Hammer vampires to Toho's Godzilla. The big screen was populated by slashers and Xenomorphs. It was a great time to be alive.

And then there were the *real* monsters.

Two television staples were *Ripley's Believe It or Not!* with the gravely voiced Jack Palance introducing each segment and *In Search Of...* hosted by Mr. Spock himself, Leonard Nimoy. Every week we were introduced to sasquatches, yeti, lake monsters, alien abductions, and the stories of lost planes, ships, and people. It was absolutely fascinating.

Keep in mind that we were introduced to the cryptids of these shows at the same time that astronauts were hanging out on Skylab and Jacques Cousteau was revealing the mysteries of the undersea world. The world was becoming a smaller place and it was inevitable that we would find all kinds of creatures if we only looked in the right spot.

Some of us never stopped looking.

There has been a recent resurgence of interest in the paranormal, UFOlogy, and cryptozoology. Cable networks host shows where people look for lake monsters or go "squatchin.'" Granted, they don't have the gravitas of Nimoy or Palance...

You hold in your hands the first volume of our two volume cryptid collection. *Hidden Menagerie Vol 1* contains 18 stories starring cryptozoological beasts of the land. Inside you will find some old friends and perhaps meet some new ones.

Enjoy!

Iceheart

Sarah Hans

White Buffalo Outpost was deserted when Lola and I arrived to investigate their radio silence. Even the mining crew's thermal suits were missing from the mud room.

"Where could they have gone?" Lola asked, gesturing to the empty compartments where six thermal suits should have rested.

"They probably had cabin fever and went for a stroll," I replied, stripping off my own suit and pushing it into a vacant compartment.

"I suppose we've seen worse." Lola slid out of her own thermal suit and shoved it into the compartment beside mine.

"Isolation does strange things to people."

"Don't we know it? I'll check the living quarters. You got command?"

"See you in five."

We turned and ventured in opposite directions down

the narrow corridor, just as we had dozens of times before over a decade of rescue missions.

The command center should have been bustling with activity, but instead I found the room silent, lights blinking automatically without human eyes to see them, a few motes of dust drifting in the air, stirred up by my boots. It smelled sterile, abandoned, as if the crew had never even existed. The outpost's desertion resonated.

I fiddled with the comm station controls, trying to get a signal through to our ship. After checking every frequency, I gave up and collapsed into the captain's chair. "Computer: captain's logs."

"Authorization required."

"Daniel Teegan, Native Mining Authorization two-six-eight-five-one."

"Thank you, Mister Teegan."

The crew's captain appeared before me, large as life. He was a tall man, with a craggy face, brown skin, black hair. I felt a pang of jealousy for his Lakota features and hated myself for still feeling such a petty emotion, even after all these years, even at my age.

The captain's voice was deep and monotonous as he

discussed the conditions on the outpost. I was exhausted after a week of sleepless nights since Lola announced her engagement to my rival. Warm and comfortable, I let the captain's droning voice lull me into dozing.

"Dan!"

I sat up, suddenly very awake. Had I heard someone calling my name, or dreamed it? Blinking sleep from my eyes, I glanced at the clock on the display. Lola and I had separated almost half an hour ago. That felt like a long time. What could be keeping her? White Buffalo Outpost was small—only five rooms, really.

I heard another sound, this time a crashing, and then a shout. No words, just a grunted sort of scream.

The emergency weapons locker under the command console was empty but for a flare gun. "Wosiliyagle," I muttered. Where was the standard-issue pistol? The flare gun would be worse than useless in such close quarters, but the thought of venturing into the unknown unarmed was worse. I slipped the flare gun and three flares into the pockets of my coveralls before leaving the command center.

"Lola?" I called, inching down the corridor. Silence had fallen over the outpost again, and I strained to hear anything that might give me a clue. By the time I reached the door at the end, the one leading to the living quarters, my heart was pounding, making the blood rush in my ears. I licked my suddenly very dry lips and pressed the button on the wall.

The door hissed open, but the lights didn't come up automatically. A foul smell hit me and I covered my nose with my free hand. "Lola?" I called again. I stood in the doorway for a few heartbeats, waiting for something to happen.

Lola came screaming toward me from out of the darkness. Her face was a rictus of pain and terror. Her arms, her legs, her face, everything was covered in blood. She barreled into me and took us both to the floor, where she struggled to rise, clawing at me in panic.

"Lola! It's me, it's Dan! What happened?" I tried to grab her as she scrambled away from me and down the hall toward the command center. I chased after her. She dove under the console.

I knelt down under the console to get to her. "Where are you hurt?" When I tried to touch her, she screamed and backed away, clutching at her neck. Blood pumped out between her fingers. Her eyes were so wide she looked like a terrified doll. "Let me get the first aid kit," I told her, but when I turned away, she grabbed my wrist and held me. I let her pull me in close. Her other hand came away from her neck and drew my face down to hers, smearing blood across my jaw. The uncovered wound was long and ragged, a second mouth that oozed blood.

She whispered only one word: "Wendigo."

She released me. I went for the first aid kit. She didn't protest or struggle when I pulled her from under the console so I could inject her with pain killers, apply coagulants, bandage her neck. My hands shook as I worked, and I talked to myself under my breath, trying to keep myself calm. Sweat poured down my forehead, obscuring my vision, and I wiped it away, smearing more blood across my face. My vision narrowed to a tunnel, and at the end of that tunnel was Lola. Her attacker was still on the station, somewhere, but I couldn't worry about him. Lola was all that mattered. All that had ever mattered.

When I was done, I sat down on the floor beside her in the disturbingly large pool of blood. The command center smelled like a butchery. "You're going to be okay, Lola."

Her eyes rolled up to look at me though the rest of her remained immobile. Green eyes, startling in contrast with the brown of her skin and the black of her hair, even more notable now with her skin so unnaturally pale. Lola Spotted Tail, the Oglala girl with green eyes. "You Blackfoot are such bad liars," she rasped.

I pressed my fingers to her lips, unable to suppress a relieved chuckle. She was well enough to make sarcastic remarks, which made the fist inside my chest unclench just a little. And she had referred to me as Blackfoot, which gave me that tingly all-over warm feeling it always did. Lola had never cared that I didn't look like one of The People. Maybe that was why I loved her. That, and the sarcasm.

"I'd tell you not to talk, but I know you Oglala aren't good at following orders," I quipped.

Lola gave a strained smile but didn't speak again. Fear shadowed her normally bright eyes.

"I'm going to call for help," I said, giving her hand a squeeze and getting up. I tried not to notice that her fingers were cold, too cold, and sticky with blood.

I went to the comm station and twirled dials, trying every frequency again. "This is Daniel Teegan at White Buffalo Outpost. SOS. SOS. Please respond."

Static was the only answer.

"We must be out of range," I told Lola, kneeling beside her again and clasping her hand in mine. "We have to get off the station, off Inyan, back to base. Nobody's coming to help. Can you walk? Never mind, I can carry you."

I hooked my arm under her shoulders and drew her to standing. Her legs wobbled and she collapsed into the captain's chair, shaking her head. Her eyes rolled about, unfocused, and her mouth moved, but she made no sound beyond a gurgle. Blood frothed on her lips.

"Get up, get up now," I ordered. I wanted to sound authoritative but my voice shook too much. I only managed to sound scared. I put my hands on her shoulders and yanked her from the chair. Hauling her toward the door, I was grateful that she had been chosen for this mission, because any of the other rescue squad members would have been too big for me to carry this way. A punch of guilt hit me so hard I had to stop walking for a moment, the breath knocked from my lungs. If I hadn't requested her as my partner, Lola wouldn't have been here in the first place. She wouldn't have been attacked, wouldn't now be staring over the precipice of death.

I couldn't let her die. I couldn't face a life without Lola, a life wracked with guilt. If Lola died, I would die too. Maybe not here on this station, but by inches, every day, until I was a ghost. She had to live.

These were the thoughts that gave me enough strength

to get us both to the mud room. I lowered Lola gently onto the bench beside our thermal suits.

"You're nearly as pale as I am," I told her, hoping to get a smile, but she didn't even look at me. I took down a thermal suit and lifted her feet into it. "You're going to have to help me here, Lola. I can't do this by myself." I managed to get the thermal suit up over her body, her arms more or less into the sleeves, though she was limp as a rag doll and much heavier.

Her hand shot out and rested against my chest, stopping me. I looked up to see her eyes wide, nostrils flared, lips parted. She was staring down the corridor. I followed her gaze to see only shadows. Moving shadows.

I heard the sound of rending steel. Whatever had attacked Lola was still on board the outpost, and it was coming for us. I drew the flare gun from my pocket and loaded it. My hands shook, but the cartridges were huge and hard to miss.

The lights flickered. I placed the flare gun in Lola's lap and drew my legs into my thermal suit, cramming my feet into the boots and shoving my arms into the sleeves. I zipped up the torso and drew on the helmet. I didn't take the time to secure the seams or lace the boots. There was no time.

I kept glancing at the shadows at the end of the corridor,

near the living quarters. As I bent to zip Lola's suit, I realized she was whispering something. And then she was screaming it.

Wendigo.

The command center behind me went dark, but I didn't turn to look. I clutched the flare gun, barely able to feel it through my gloves, and sidled toward the airlock. I punched a button and the airlock door slid open. "Lola! Go!" I shouted, aiming the flare gun at the roiling shadows, prepared to fire and bail.

The creature that stepped into the corridor was lit only by the emergency lights. In the soft yellow glow, it stood at least two meters tall, but it was so skinny I could make out its ribs. Its face had once been human, but it was now elongated, more like that of a wolf, with huge fangs bursting from its mouth. Its arms were long and grotesque, fingers tipped with deadly curved claws. Dark hair clung to its body in uneven patches, and between its legs there dangled a shriveled member that suggested it may once have been a man. It brought with it the reek of rotten meat and death.

It lunged for me, its mouth twisted in what might have been a grimace or a smile.

I fired the flare just as Lola lurched to her feet and shoved me into the airlock. The door slid shut with a hiss, separating me from her.

"Lola!" I screamed, pounding my fist against the door entry. It required a key code, and in my thermal suit my fingers were too bulky to enter the code. I shoved the flare gun into my pocket and started to pull off my right glove.

Lola appeared in the window. She was pale, but her eyes were fierce, burning in the orange light of the flare. She mouthed words. "I don't understand!" I yelled.

She mouthed the words again. This time I could make them out: "Heart of ice."

And then she was gone.

The creature appeared in the window. Up close, I could see that it was neither grimacing nor smiling, but that it had, instead, eaten away its own lips, lips now darkened with Lola's blood.

I scrambled for the outer door and onto the surface of Inyan. The wind howled like the souls of the damned, tugging at me with the force of a hurricane. I paused in the doorway, looking back, wondering whether the creature could follow me into the icy wind without a thermal suit. How could it? Nothing could survive such extreme temperatures. Nothing…human.

Wendigo. I thought about my grandfather and the stories of The People, stories I'd resented because they couldn't be mine, not with my blond hair and blue eyes, not without a Lakota name to give me legitimacy. The word was familiar and brought to mind a monster that had once been a man, a creature corrupted by tasting the blood of other men until all that remained was a ravenous husk fueled by a cold need, an empty yearning, a hunger. A creature with, legends said, a heart of ice.

The door shook, and a dent appeared from the inside. I jumped back; the wendigo had somehow managed to breach the airlock. I wasn't sure whether it could get through the reinforced steel door, but I didn't want to stick around and find out. Flicking on my headlamp, I turned and ran for the garage. Sweat blinded me and I tasted salt on my lips, salt and something else: Lola's blood running from my cheeks into my mouth. I gagged, stumbling, struggling to get back up, the thermal suit cumbersome.

I imagined that, behind me, I could hear steel bending and twisting beneath the screaming wind, and the sound pushed me forward.

I staggered to the garage and heaved open the door. The rover was parked just inside. I climbed on board and put the flare gun on the seat beside me—what should have been Lola's seat—and felt relief flood my aching limbs. Surely the rover could outrun a man, even one that had become a monster, especially one exposed to the frostbite-inducing cold of the moon's surface.

I brought up the display on my helmet with a flick of my eyes. "Daniel Teegan to Thunderbird. SOS."

"Thunderbird here."

I guffawed with joy. "Iron Cloud? Oh man, you have no idea how good it is to hear your voice!"

"Why the SOS? What's happening?"

"I need immediate evacuation. I'll be at the rendezvous ASAP."

"What about Lola?"

"No Lola. She...didn't make it." I swallowed hard against the lump that had risen in my throat. "Teegan out."

"Wait, what's happening? You can't just tell me Lola's..."

"Just meet me at the rendezvous! Teegan out!" Another flick of my eyes disabled the radio. I bit back tears. I couldn't afford to think about Lola right now. I couldn't let her sacrifice be for nothing.

I turned the key in the ignition and the rover's engine roared to life. The headlights illuminated a twisted silhouette in the garage doorway, blocking my path. Shuddering, I lowered my head, pressed the throttle to the floor, and then released the brake. The rover surged forward, snapping my head back, and charged toward the monster.

I was counting on the rover to make mincemeat of the wendigo. Instead, the creature crouched and affected a leap that would have been the envy of every professional lacrosse player in the Sioux Nation. I watched in the rearview as it landed nimbly behind the rover, dwindling as the vehicle carried me away.

I gunned the rover to its maximum speed, grateful for the smooth ground that offered no obstacles. The GPS in my helmet overlaid my path with a map, guiding me to the rendezvous coordinates.

Something heavy landed on the roof of the rover with a horrible crunch. The wendigo's upside-down face appeared in the windshield. I slammed on the brakes, expecting the wendigo's inertia to carry it forward as the rover stopped. But I underestimated the monster's strength. It held on, dropping down onto the hood to stare at me through the glass.

The wendigo punched the windshield, and though the glass was industrial space-grade, stars appeared. I screamed and reached for my only weapon, the flare gun on the passenger seat.

A second punch made larger cracks appear, less like stars and more like leggy spiders. Now cursing with fear, certain that my death was imminent—only a quarter klick from the rendezvous, my GPS assured me—I fumbled with the flare gun. My fingers in the suit were too bulky to operate the gun, and the remaining flares were in the pocket of my coveralls.

Panting, I put the flare gun in my left hand and pushed off my right glove. I pulled my right hand into the thermal suit to dig in my coveralls for the flares.

The wendigo's third punch cracked the windshield so completely the monster was obscured from view. One more punch and he would be through. I maneuvered around the flare gun to open the door with my left hand and rolled out of the rover onto the frozen ground.

I pulled myself up and ran. I knew the wendigo followed me though I couldn't hear its footfalls over the wind. I found a flare in my pocket with my right hand and then shoved the hand back through the thermal suit's sleeve.

Timing would be everything. My hand would survive only a few seconds in the bitter cold. I would have to load the gun and fire it before frostbite set in.

And I would have to trust that Lola was right about the

wendigo's heart of ice.

I jammed the flare into the gun and turned. The thermal suit was voluminous, not designed for sudden movement; my legs became tangled and I fell onto my back. The wendigo loomed above me. My hand was already starting to ache from the cold. I raised the flare gun and squeezed the trigger.

The flare struck the wendigo's chest and buried itself in the monster's ribs. A bright red light glowed from behind its flesh. It roared, a sound equal parts animal howl and human scream, staggering back from me to claw at its chest.

I scrambled to my feet and watched as the wendigo thrashed and groaned, dying in convulsions.

I drew my right arm back into the thermal suit, my fingers burning. I waited until the wendigo stopped thrashing. A few moments later, the flare in its chest sputtered out. In the distance, I could see the lights on the Thunderbird winking and flashing.

When I arrived at the rendezvous and the crew came out to meet me, they found me dragging the wendigo's corpse with my one good hand. They bundled me onto one stretcher and the wendigo onto another. We were wheeled into separate bays. Medical personnel stripped away my thermal suit and then I felt a quick pinch at my neck. A warm, languorous feeling spread through my body and my concerns about the wendigo became fuzzy.

I don't remember much after that until a few days later, when Paul Iron Cloud entered the medical bay. He glowered, dark eyes smoldering beneath heavy black brows.

"Did you even try to save her?"

"Nice to see you too, Iron Cloud," I said from the bed. My voice was raspy after days without use. I waved at him with the handless stump that capped my right arm.

"Answer the question."

"What do you think?" His accusation should probably have made me feel sad, or annoyed, or anything, but I just felt numb. He smelled strange, like a fresh steak, and my stomach churned.

"I think you left her to die." There were tears in his eyes. His mouth was a tight pucker.

I returned his glare with equal force. We'd never gotten along, because two men who love the same woman never do. He'd blame me for Lola's death no matter what I said. "Think what you like."

"Native Mining wants to celebrate you as a hero, you

know. They're planning a Naming Ceremony and everything." Paul's eyes bored into me.

"I don't want a name," I growled.

"The crew families insist on it. Well, except Moon Walker's."

I flinched. Adam Moon Walker had been the astrophysicist aboard White Buffalo Outpost. The wendigo's DNA was a match for his. The nurses who gossiped over my bed whispered that he'd failed the psychological tests for living in the outpost's isolated conditions, but he'd been sent anyway. Whether a mere clerical error or malicious incompetence was responsible, nobody knew. The rest of the crew had been found in the mine shaft. They'd been trying to hide from the creature that had once been Moon Walker, presumably, and all that remained of them were clean-picked bones surrounded by the shredded remains of their thermal suits. Their families had sued Native Mining over the failed psychological tests and now, according to the nurses, they got whatever they wanted. Which, I guess, included canonizing me.

"I don't want a name," I repeated.

"Oh come on now, Teegan," Paul sneered, "we all know how much you want a name. You've whined about it your entire life. Poor little white boy, with his blond hair and blue eyes, never really Lakota. No matter what they name you, some of us will know you're not really one of The People. How could you be when you let Lola die?"

He stormed out, the dramatic effect of his exit somewhat lessened by the soft hiss of the door closing behind him. I retched over the railing of my bed onto the floor, my stomach once again rejecting the freeze-dried food, an action which summoned several nurses to swarm my bed.

A few hours later, Chief Red Star appeared at my bedside. "Choosing a name for you is proving difficult," he told me. "The families can't agree."

"I don't want a name." I gritted my teeth so hard they made a scraping sound. The noise reminded me of the wendigo rending the outpost's steel doors and a shudder shook my whole body.

Red Star patted my hand. He smelled salty and smoky, like beef jerky. "It's time, son. You've waited so long for this. You've earned the honor, and you wouldn't turn away a kind gesture by the families of those you avenged, would you? So tell me what you think: Daniel White Buffalo? Wendigo Slayer? Personally I like Blue Eyes, myself, though it doesn't reference your heroism…"

I stared at the knitting stump of my hand and thought of Lola's last words. My name had been an albatross around my neck my entire life, but maybe now it could be a reminder. A reminder of failure. A reminder of sacrifice.

"Iceheart," I said in a tone that allowed for no compromise, no argument.

Red Star blinked at me. "Daniel Iceheart. Has a nice ring to it."

"No," I said, flexing the nonexistent fingers of my amputated hand. "Just Iceheart."

The Chief nodded, sorrow flickering across his face. "I'll tell the families."

He got up and lumbered toward the door. I lay there, staring down at my wrist. The doctors would offer me a prosthetic, and I already knew I would refuse it. How could I walk around pretending I was whole when Lola was dead?

"See you for the Naming Ceremony tomorrow, Mister Teegan."

"Iceheart," I corrected him.

He hesitated in the doorway. "Lola Spotted Tail's death was the fault of the wendigo, you know," he said. "You can't blame yourself."

"Of course I can," I snarled. "She died on my watch, under my command. She was my responsibility."

He bowed his head. "The wendigo had a heart of ice, not you. No matter what your name." I let him have the last word as the door hissed shut behind him.

In my chest, my heart felt cold and hard, like a frozen stone. I remembered the taste of Lola's blood on my lips and shivered.

Please Don't Feed The Howler

Frances Pauli

Jenny Munch began feeding the animals the day after the visiting park ranger spoke to her class. She'd listened to the lecture with only slightly more attentiveness than her classmates, but overnight the ideas he planted sparked and festered until she woke that Saturday morning certain the birds and squirrels on her parent's farm would die of starvation if she didn't supplement their diets.

The sum total of her hoarded allowance, originally destined to purchase a party dress from the department store, went straight into Hank's pocket at the Feed 'n Farm, and Jenny hauled home a twenty pound sack of cracked corn, three bags of straight millet, and some lard.

She spent the better part of her weekend building feeders, melting lard and arguing with her mother about her newest obsession.

"Jenny, the smell!"

"Ranger Phillips told us that the winter months are an

incredibly fragile time for local species."

"Does it have to be in my cooking pots?"

"Every citizen can do their part, Mom. Ranger Phillips said we can make a difference."

Her mother had scowled at that and then made it perfectly clear that Jenny's neck would be on the chopping block if any of her fragile freeloaders destroyed the garden come spring. Then she'd wandered from the room, casting about for Jenny's father or "anyone with a little sense."

By Sunday evening Jenny had six bird feeders complete with suet cakes scattered around the property and a plywood platform at the fence line overflowing with cracked corn. She pestered her father into digging an old pair of binoculars out of the attic and spent her family TV time perched backwards on the couch trying desperately to see squirrels in the dark.

That night she slept with the binoculars around her neck, and she woke fifteen minutes before normal and scrambled into her snow boots and warm coat without changing out of her pajamas. Jenny slipped past the kitchen, ignored the thick scent of breakfast and squeezed out the front door before her mother could call her back.

The grass crunched under her rubber soles, frosty and

promising worse weather soon. Jenny hustled to the first feeder with her enthusiasm loaded into her steps and spooked a flurry of small birds from their own morning meal. They'd found it! The birds had discovered the suet, and now, Jenny had fulfilled her part as an environmentally conscious citizen. She hugged her arms around her body and skipped in place before stalking the second feeder with much greater care.

Her soft steps earned her a peek at four sparrows and a nuthatch and put an even larger wiggle of pride in her belly. At the third feeder, she watched a crow worry away a ring of tiny finches, the forth had more sparrows, and at the fifth, Jenny discovered a massacre.

She felt the weight of it in her boots. A sick crawly feeling evicted her morning's victory, and she stared open-mouthed at the sea of plucked feathers, the slashes of blood painted across the grass, and the bits of bird, the torn wing, still dangling from the edge of her handmade feeder. Something had ripped them all to pieces.

The cold spread from her toes upward.

Her legs shook inside her flannel pajamas, rattled the snow boots against one another. Something ate her birds. She'd drawn them in to the millet, and then...

She thought of the squirrel feeder then, the platform at the fence line, right up against the forest's edge. There was one more bird feeder, the one closest to the house, and Jenny thought of checking it first. Perhaps her mother would catch her there, and she wouldn't be able to hike out to the fence line after breakfast. She looked at her toes, at the patch of frosty grass that didn't have red smears across it, and a stab of guilt prickled at her.

It wouldn't hurt to check. There was probably nothing wrong, nothing gory at the squirrel platform. Some neighbor's cat had simply seized the opportunity her feeder provided. She'd have to plant catnip on the far side of the field perhaps, or convince her parents to let her get a dog.

Jenny skirted well around the mess, but her eyes flicked in enough times to keep her stomach tumbling. She'd never liked the sight of blood. Not even her own. By the time she worked her way out to the pasture, she didn't expect she'd be able to keep the bacon down this morning. Mom would be suspicious.

She ducked through the rails and headed across the pasture. The forest crept right up to the field there, dark and full of old, deciduous growth. Halfway across she knew something had happened. The ground around the feeder looked wrong.

The grass made lumps where it had been smooth, long trenches gouged in nearly frozen ground. Like someone had plowed. Or something had clawed the earth to shreds. She didn't need to see the blood. Whatever creature had been lured to her corn had suffered a grizzly end.

Jenny turned her back on the scene, turned her eyes toward home, and the forest howled behind her. The sound bugled from the brush and shook the last of the corn from the feeder. She heard it raining to the ground. She heard it, as she ran for home as fast as her trembling legs could carry her.

She made it three days before they noticed she'd lost interest. Her mother reminded her on the way to school on Thursday. "Jenny, you haven't filled your feeders in a few days."

Jenny grunted and hurried for the bus stop with her book bag dangling from one shoulder. When her father got home that night, he remembered the birds as well.

"Jenny, that feeder by the house is all out of seed. I think you'd better refill them tonight."

"Can't I do it in the morning?" She shuffled her feet and eyed the stairway, then the window behind the couch where the last shreds of daylight leaked away.

"No. Do it now. There's enough light yet."

"But—"

"This is your responsibility, young lady, and it was your idea. Once you start feeding them, they come to expect it. Animals become dependent on a regular, readily available food source."

"Okay." She took a step toward the staircase, and her father put down his paper. "Now?"

"Now."

She dragged her feet getting her coat on and earned another over the paper scowl. Outside, she eyed the dropping sun like it was out to get her. Then she bolted for the barn, debating in her mind the whole way. If she waited in here for a bit and then just filled the feeder by the house, they might think she'd done them all. Somehow, Jenny felt her father would see through the deception. She filled the scoop with cracked corn and took a deep breath.

There was still enough light.

She ran across the pasture, slowing only when she could make out the lumps of twisted ground at the feeder's base. No blood stained the grass today, and no little bodies either. Maybe, she'd imagined them before. She hadn't come this close, not after seeing the mess at the bird feeder. Jenny slunk up to the platform

and dumped her scoop, spilling a golden waterfall to the wood.
The ruts could have been made by a deer's hooves, even.

Jenny told herself that and didn't look at the marks again.
She dumped her corn and backed away from the feeder with a
little prayer for the squirrels. It could have been a deer, in fact,
that tore up the ground. She warmed to the idea as she walked.
And a neighbor's cat could have gotten the birds, too.

She filled the horrible bird feeder first. Here the blood
still showed against the grass, dark now. Unless you knew what
had happened, it might be anything. Jenny focused on pouring
the seed and had just started for the next in line when the forest
rattled back at the fence line. She turned, heart pounding,
in time to see the deer emerge. Jenny let out a breath, let her
shoulders drop and watched the doe approach the corn, gently,
each step placed with careful silence.

A howl erupted from the trees. The deer leapt into the
air, hit the ground and bounded up again. It sprinted for the
trees farther down, well beyond the feeding platform and the
spilled corn, and Jenny watched it as if she were in a trance.
Her chest pounded and the bag of birdseed slipped between her
fingers. The howl came again, a strangled bugle from the edge of
the trees. The branches shifted, and a dark shape slipped between

them. Big. Jenny saw that much even from across the pasture. Black and bigger than a cougar even. More like a bear, but then, bears never made a sound like that.

She backed up, stumbled over her sack of seeds and squatted without really looking, fished for it with her fingers while the trees rippled beyond the fence. The deer vanished back into the woods, and the black thing followed it, crashing and howling as it went. Shaggy. Black and big.

Jenny waited until she couldn't see it, couldn't hear anything any longer. Then she bolted for the feeder by the house, dumped the rest of the seed into it, and left the empty bag on the ground before fleeing indoors. When she'd shucked her coat in the entryway and caught her breath enough to stand fully upright, she came nose to nose with her father.

"Something after you?" He grinned. His paper tucked under his left arm, a neat roll of news that had nothing to do with terrible black monsters.

"I think...there's...a bear."

"We haven't had a bear in years, Jenny. Too many people building by the woods."

"Saw it. A big black one." She held her arm straight out at her shoulder's height. "Something ate my birds."

"Probably the neighbor's cat." He father frowned and rubbed his chin. "If a bear has wandered in, we should let the local authorities know."

"Do you think they'll come to trap it?"

"Possibly. If it's coming in this close, then it might pose a danger."

Jenny felt the relief like a flood. It thawed the fear in her belly. She smiled for real, for the first time in three days.

"You'll still keep those feeders full, young lady." Her father said. "Bear or not."

"But—"

"Just do it before school."

"O-Okay."

"And if you need help…"

"Yes?"

"You can ask your mother."

He winked at her, and Jenny tried to let it soothe her. She tried to believe the black thing in the woods was a bear, that it would leave her alone if she went out in the mornings, but she already planned to skip the squirrel platform. Maybe just keep the one by the house full, the one that her father would notice.

If the authorities tried to trap the bear, and then they saw it too…

Jenny smiled for her father and nodded, but in her mind she saw the branches rippling. She saw the black animal chasing the doe, shaggier than a bear and a lot more massive. She saw it, and she heard the sound it made, the howl that Jenny knew had not come from anything half as normal as a bear.

Snow fell overnight. The feeder still overflowed with seed when she checked it, and so Jenny bolted for school without worry and spent one entire day thinking about ordinary things that had nothing to do with blood or howling things. She waded home through the snow with only a quick, guilty glance in the direction of the pasture.

The family dinner passed in blissful ordinariness, and it wasn't until after the pie was served that her father chose to spoil it completely.

"Your bear took down a deer last night." He used the side of his fork to cut a bite of pie, and took his time disposing of it before he continued. "Wilson next door found a chunk of it on his property. Chewed to shreds, he said."

"Bill!" Jenny's mother objected to talk of chewed deer at her table. She tutted and made obvious eyes in Jenny's direction.

"Jenny saw it," her father said. "A big bear on the

property. Wilson called the Fish and Game."

"Oh. Well be sure to tell them to keep out of my gardens. Jenny, don't you like the pie?"

"It's good." She stared at the ruby cherries spilling across her plate and imagined what chewed to shreds looked like. "Can I be excused?"

"If you like. Can't have them tromping all over the gardens, Bill. Bill?"

Jenny and her father locked gazes. They stared over the top of the pie and for the first time, perhaps, completely understood one another.

"Did you fill the feeders today?" He cut another bite of pie and lifted it in the air.

"Just the one by the house."

"Good." He nodded, but a grim light had settled in his eyes. "Best to leave them for awhile then. No sense risking it."

"Okay."

She carried her plate to the kitchen, dumped the untouched slice of pie into the trash and stared out the window above the sink. A small bird had found her feeder. It bounced atop the mound of millet, pecking merrily between each hop. She didn't have to fill them now. Good. She didn't want to, couldn't bear the thought of tramping through the snow all the way out to the squirrel platform.

But as she rinsed her plate, another thought surfaced. Something her father had said the day before. Something about dependence and a readily available food source. Had the howling thing already learned where the food could be found? Jenny eyed the bird and felt the quiver in her stomach again. If it came to her platform tonight and found no one eating there, would it go hungry or go hunting?

She didn't imagine a wild animal would come much closer than that fence line. Animals were born with a natural fear of man. Ranger Phillips had said so. But the chewed up birds had been a lot closer than the fence, and no matter what her father said about bears, Jenny wasn't certain that the black thing she'd seen would have a natural fear of anything.

The howling thing had caught the deer, had left a chewed up hunk of it at the Wilson's. Did that mean it wasn't really hungry at all? If it wasn't, Jenny didn't want to know. She dried her plate without looking, stared out the window at the empty feeder. The bird had flown away, she was sure. Nothing spooked it, and nothing, not a bear or a howling thing, moved against the snow outside.

"It's not your fault, Jenny." Her father spoke over his paper, but she couldn't see him. She stared out the living room window, sat backwards on the couch, and imagined shadows creeping around the yard. "A few birds and a squirrel are not enough to lure a bear in like this. It must have been something else. Someone built on his territory and uprooted him."

Except he hadn't killed anything until she'd put the feeders out.

"That dog of Wilson's was getting old," her father continued.

The chickens hadn't been old, nor had the two lambs at the Kent's place.

"Jenny?"

"Yes?"

"They'll trap it before the week is out, you watch."

But the traps had been there for a week already, and the howling thing never went near them.

"Jenny?"

It did come near her house, however. Jenny had seen the shadows move. She'd caught a glimpse of shaggy, black hair between the fence posts, and even once, behind the barn. The howling thing teased her, made sure she knew why it had come and what it wanted. In the end, it wanted her.

"Jenny?"

"I think I'll go to bed early."

"On Saturday?"

"I have a project to work on tomorrow."

Her father grunted and lifted his newspaper barrier back into place. She hadn't lied. Not exactly. Jenny had made a decision, after the Wilson's dog was found. She'd fashioned a plan when she caught the Howler creeping in behind the barn, and if she told her father about it, he'd lock her in her room forever. But the howling thing needed to die. The fish and game men couldn't catch it—they meant to trap a bear. Jenny wasn't even sure that they'd be able to see it.

Maybe, only she could see it.

If so, then only Jenny could kill it. She had most of the corn left, and a lot of seed. If she lured in enough animals… Her father kept an old shotgun in the barn. Once, when Jenny had been much younger, she'd seen him use it on a coyote. She knew which drawer he kept the shells in, too.

All she had to do was hide. All she had to do was let it get close enough. Jenny stood, but dragged her feet on the way to the stairs. She looked up the long slope and imagined being alone outside in the dark. Was the Howler out there now? She thought it was, and she thought for certain, it would be waiting for her tomorrow.

She'd poured the rest of the corn onto the platform and topped it with one of the bags of millet just to be sure. Just in case the Howler really wanted birds. Her pocket bulged with the shells she'd stolen, and her fingers continually dipped in to check on them, to make certain they were still there. The snow glowed ghost white under a half moon now. Jenny had put the seed out before dark. She'd eaten while the birds ate, and she'd climbed up to her bedroom under the pretense of an early night's sleep.

Her window opened onto the wraparound porch roof. A trellis climbed up the side of that, and less than an hour after her parents had also gone to bed, Jenny searched the barn for the shotgun that should have been right inside the door.

She heard the Howler before she found the weapon. It bugled in the distance, not the sound of a bear at all. Her chest squeezed, and ice flowed beneath her skin. Jenny shivered. She turned left and right, watched the doors on both ends of the barn as if the black beast would spring through them at any second.

Instead, she found the shotgun.

He'd moved it to the other door, leaned it up against the wheelbarrow like any other tool. She forced her feet to un-stick and slipped along the stall fronts to fetch the gun. Two shells slid into it easily enough. She'd seen her father work the catch and knew how to do that much. What worried her was how close she'd have to get. How far could a shotgun reach? How fast could she reload it, if she missed?

The howling came again before Jenny left the barn. It still sounded distant, came from the direction of the squirrel platform. Right where she wanted it, and still, her stomach clenched over and over again. She hesitated in the barn door, an ordinary schoolgirl with a shotgun under one arm and a monster lurking in the night outside.

She waited until the echoes of the howl had died before stepping into the open. The snow had fallen steadily for the last few days, and the farm lay under a deep blanket. She'd spent the afternoon scraping herself a thin pathway to the fence, and her steps now fell in silence. The only sound she made was the faint whisper of her sleeves against the body of her jacket, whish, whish, so softly that even Jenny had to strain to hear it.

She held the gun at her waist, pointing ahead and wobbling a lot more than she'd imagined. The barrel was heavy, and not at all as steady as it had been in her father's hands. What would happen if she missed? Somehow, that possibility hadn't seemed real before this. Suddenly, the madness of her plan clarified.

Jenny stopped walking and stared at the fence ahead. The partial moon lit up the snow, and the trees behind it were a black swath. She'd never see the thing inside those trees. It would have to come into the open. The feeder waited out there, but would it be enough to draw the howling thing out? What if there were no birds tonight? Her breath fogged the air, puffed in icy clouds as she pondered it. She should probably just sneak back into bed.

The snow behind her crunched. A low growl rumbled through her boots and up, vibrating her knees. Jenny turned around as slowly as she could. She swung the gun ahead of her, led with the barrel and stopped cold halfway around. The howling thing crouched beside the pathway she'd scraped. It hunkered between Jenny and the barn, a lump of shaggy black fur twice the size of any bear, or maybe, alone in the darkness, it just seemed that big.

Either way, no bear looked like that. No bear had pinpoint red eyes and two long horns curving backwards where it's ears should be. She raised the gun, just like her father had done. The Howler opened its jaws, and the night exploded with the sound, the keening bugle.

Jenny's finger found the triggers. The Howler's shoulders shifted back and forth. She squeezed too hard. The shotgun jerked in her arms and knocked her backwards. She stumbled, but she saw the howling thing recoil. She heard it screech, louder than the howl even, loud enough to wake the dead.

She stayed on her feet, backed up a step and steadied herself. The howling thing fell over, crashed to the snow without another sound. Its sides heaved, a moving mountain of fur against the snow, up and down. Still breathing. Still living.

Jenny heard the sounds from the house now, the door slamming. Footsteps. Her hands shook, but she wrestled the shotgun open. The hot shells tumbled to the snow, and Jenny fished in her pocket for the next pair.

The Howler grunted, and she slid the first shell into place. It heaved to its feet again, and Jenny dropped the second shell into the snow.

She stared ahead. The Howler's head lowered. It's eyes squinted back at her. She'd never find the shell in time. The snow was too deep. Did a shotgun fire with only one? The Howler growled at her, and Jenny snapped the barrel closed. She raised the half loaded weapon, and listened to the footsteps crunching through the snow. Her father would go to the barn. He'd go for the gun she'd already stolen.

The Howler's body lowered. Jenny opened her mouth to scream. She raised the gun at the same time it leapt for her, and her shouting drowned in another bone-chilling howl. Jenny never pulled the trigger. The weapon dropped from her hands, and the night filled with the flashing motion of black claws and snow white teeth.

Ruth Daniels smacked her bubble gum and doodled on her notebook with a ball point pen. She'd drawn a sea of hearts, at least four perfect eyes, and the school mascot to cover up the name of the boy she'd liked last semester. Mrs. Kent stood at the front of the class. She clapped her hands over the breast of her herringbone suit and looked far more pleased than any middle aged high school teacher had a right too.

"...Our special guest today," she said. Her voice droned like an old record, stuck on a single word. "And I hope you'll give her your full attention."

Ruth didn't give Mrs. Kent her full attention, and she hardly saw reason to extend that courtesy to a guest speaker, whatever the topic. Today's torture had something to do with ecology. She'd been doodling during that part of the introduction, and she blew off the rest of it now. A corner of her notepad was still bare, and she began lining out a pair of fat, kissing lips.

"How every citizen can make a difference," Mrs. Kent finished.

Ruth smacked her gum again, blew a fat bubble and looked up just as the classroom door opened. The guest speaker limped in, and Ruth's bubble popped loudly. She focused, perhaps for the first time in her academic history, on the woman at the front of the class, and nearly swallowed her bubblegum.

Scars covered the woman's face. Her left cheek sank in like a skeleton's where some reconstructive surgery had gone very wrong. One of her eyes stared like an empty stone, probably glass, definitely not natural. The other one, however, moved constantly, darting from student to student and making contact with each one. That eye settled on Ruth, froze her like a deer in the headlights.

The woman raised one arm, and the class fell silent. She had fingers missing, more scars twining up to vanish inside her sleeve. Her voice, when she spoke, came out with effort, a harsh, rasping whisper that had the entire class suddenly, fully fixated, entranced by the horrible picture she made, by the pain leaking through every word.

"Good afternoon," she said.

Ruth scooted forward on her chair. Leaned her elbows onto the forgotten notebook.

"My name is Jenny Munch."

Holiday Hunt

Joette M. Rozanski

"Tonight will be perfect, won't it?" Marguerite asked as she squeezed Marie's hand. She leaned forward and patted Jeremy's left shoulder. "How lovely Leona found you, Jeremy! We haven't had a proper guest for two years!"

Jeremy glanced at Leona, who drove the black sedan across the long road that curled through the Michigan countryside. Leona was a tall blonde woman whose sable coat and hat made her pale skin look like alabaster. She smiled at Jeremy, then returned her attention to the road.

"I'm flattered," Jeremy said to Marguerite. "I'm grateful that your family invited me to your holiday dinner."

Marguerite shrieked with laughter and sat back again. Jeremy thought the twins were odd, but he tried his best to make friends with them. After all, they were Leona's little sisters. Both girls had long dark hair and big brown eyes. They wore matching silver fox coats and black leather boots. Marguerite was an inch or so taller than Marie; otherwise, the girls were identical.

Jeremy's gaze swept across the thick snow that covered

northern Michigan - so pure and white, tinged with the slightest hint of pink from the setting sun. In the near distance, tall fir trees, their tips wreathed with tiny stars, swayed with the breeze. Something long and dark slipped between them.

Jeremy blinked and stared hard at the creature. Wolverines had been seen of late in the Michigan wilderness and he wondered if one had just run across the road. The animal's gait seemed too awkward for a dog or wolf.

Marie understood her twin sister's glee. The holiday just wasn't the same without a guest to entertain the family and now they had one. Grandmama would spend the evening staring out the window, her face lifted to Our Lady, her mouth curved up into a crescent.

She turned around and seized Marguerite's cold hand. Her dark eyes shone above her silver fox collar.

"Yes," Marie assured her. "We will have the best time ever. I can feel it."

She looked past her dim reflection in the glass beside her and knew she spoke true. Night loped across the sky, its heavy black coat covering the sun's face. A thrill of anticipation shot through her body, a sensation so strong that she kicked her boots against Jeremy's seat.

He didn't seem to mind; he just smiled at Leona and shook his head. Marie lowered her window, allowing the clean cold wind to blow against their faces.

"Hear that?" she cried. "Hear the dogs?"

Leona threw back her head and laughed. "Dogs, dearest? Or coyotes? Aren't we supposed to blame them for the music now?"

They grew quiet, listening to the chorus of howling that wavered through the night. A single human-like scream split the cold air; Jeremy looked startled, but didn't say anything.

Leona laughed again. "You can hear the strangest things in the Upper Peninsula. Isn't that right, girls?"

Marie stifled a giggle and poked Marguerite, who poked her back.

"Yes, Leona," Marie said. "Very strange."

Jeremy was glad when the ride finally came to an end; the twins in the back seat seemed creepier by the minute, especially when they began howling along with the dogs or wolves or whatever they were.

The car's tires squealed across the snow as Leona made a hard right onto the narrow road that led to her grandmother's house. Her estate lay far from any town or village; the surrounding fields were covered with velvety, pale bracken, and well-grown saplings. The main house and outbuildings were constructed of gray fieldstone, as was the low fence that ringed the property. A great iron gate swung open as their car approached, and Jeremy smiled to see the wide, bare windows filled with cheery yellow light.

Uncle Renard, who lived with the family matriarch, met them at the door.

"Everybody else is here," he announced, running his big-knuckled hand over his bald head. "They're with Mother in the parlor." He extended his hand to Jeremy. "Welcome to our home, young fellow."

"Thanks," Jeremy said. "I'm happy to be here."

Without waiting to remove their coats, Marguerite and Marie ran shouting into the great-room. A freshly-cut pine tree stood there, its branches haphazardly strung with tinsel, which dripped onto dusty and crumpled boxes which they knew were empty. The girls laughed at them, the family joke, and bounded into the parlor.

Nearly thirty relatives from as many states sat on chairs ranged around the small room. The pink-and-white striped wallpaper made their long faces rosy and teased auburn highlights from their black hair.

Mother and Father sat near the cabinet with all the china dogs shimmering against the glass. They nodded to their daughters. They had arrived earlier with the main course.

Grandmama sat in a rocking-chair near the fireplace. A few thin streamers of flame burned blue and green across the logs, their colors reflected in her dark eyes every time she swung her head toward them. She was dressed in black,: her silver hair hung down her back like a cape. Long nails, white as milk, curved from her slim fingertips.

Several relatives frowned as Marie and Marguerite ran past them, but Grandmama's lips stretched into a wide smile. They were her favorites, because they were most like her.

"Come here, my little ones," she said. They went to her and she hugged them.

Mother came and helped them with their coats; they twirled around, showing off their lacy dresses with the enormous satin bows. But Grandmama didn't seem to notice.

"We have a guest," she whispered. Her breath smelled coppery, like pennies. "We must be especially nice to him. Leona has intentions."

Marie and Marguerite glanced around the parlor, then saw Jeremy sitting beside Leona beneath the soft light from the crystal chandelier. He was tall and sallow and wore a blue suit that bled black creases. A bright smile was fixed upon his face as he gazed around at family and made the occasional remark to Leona.

"He's got quite long legs, hasn't he?" Marie asked. "I bet he's a good runner."

Before the twins could say anything more, Uncle Renard stepped into the parlor and announced that dinner was ready. They trooped into the dining room—except for Grandmama, who remained near the fireplace. A roast goose, surrounded by dishes and bowls filled with traditional fixings, lay upon the long oaken dining table. Marguerite and Marie sat at a smaller table with several young cousins, but they didn't mind. Next year, when they were thirteen years old, they'd they would sit with the adults.

Hardly anyone spoke as they devoured the goose with much clatter of china and silverware. Vegetables, relishes, salads, and sweets were ignored. Uncle Renard asked Jeremy about his family but, upon discovering that he hadn't any, left him alone. A few cousins smiled and nodded at Leona, silently congratulating her on her good work.

After several minutes of quiet, Jeremy asked, "Where's your Grandmother?"

Leona didn't look at him. "Grandmama finds talking tiresome. You'll see her at the sleigh ride."

"Sleigh ride?" Jeremy asked, all smiles. "That sounds like fun."

"Poor goose," Marguerite whispered to Marie, who giggled.

Jeremy turned his bright smile on them.

"I think your sisters have a secret," he said to Leona; he winked at Marie. "Little girls love having secrets, don't they?"

"Oh, yes," Marie said. "We have lots."

"Why don't you tell me one? I'm very good at keeping secrets."

"Do you like fairy tales?"

Marguerite shrieked and punched Marie's arm.

Jeremy blinked, confused. "I...I suppose..."

"My favorite is Little Red Riding Hood," Marie said. "The wolf is dressed like her grandmother and gobbles her up."

"That's not how it goes," Jeremy said, seriously. "The

wood-cutter arrives in time to save her."

Marie shrugged. "That was a lie. The wolf killed him, too, but since he'd already eaten Red Riding Hood and her grandmother, shared him with the rest of the pack."

"The wolf is more of a dog," Marguerite explained, "and the pack is made up of dog people. And they all live here in Michigan."

Jeremy scowled and Leona touched his arm. "The girls have vivid imaginations," she said.

"Gruesome is more like it."

He decided to change the subject. "I noticed that your Christmas presents were still wrapped, even though today is December 31st. Are you waiting for more family members to arrive?"

"We're not too fond of Christmas," Uncle Renard said. "We like New Year's better."

"And solstice," Marie added. "The Holly King dies and the berries are his blood."

Jeremy grimaced.

"Gloomy little thing, aren't you? Besides, solstice is over."

"Not for us. We celebrate all month. The hungry sun eats the night and becomes stronger and stronger. So do we."

Jeremy nodded as if he understood but said nothing more. He heard barking in the distance and saw some sort of canine run past the dining room window.

The adults passed bottles of wine around the table and became quite merry. Marie loved watching their faces grow longer, their eyes greener, their nails sharper. Our Lady sang to them from the sky, offering them the freedom of the wild, the laughter that shattered human boundaries...and bones.

Another hour flew by, and then Uncle Renard shoved his chair back, stood up, and shouted, "Now! Now is the time!"

Uncles, aunts, parents, and cousins pounded the table with their fists and yelled at the tops of their voices. Jeremy seemed surprised at such enthusiasm; he hesitated, then clapped his hands together like a child.

Mother walked over to Marguerite and Marie and, using her sternest voice, said, "No riding for you two, not with the colds you've just gotten over. You may watch from the library window."

They knew better than to protest. Everyone else bundled into coats and boots and then, with much coarse laughter, tramped outside.

Leona tucked a sprig of holly behind Jeremy's left ear and

kissed him on the lips.

"My Holly King," she breathed.

"With garnish," Marie whispered to Marguerite, who slapped her hand against her mouth to stifle her laughter.

Waving goodbye to Jeremy, the girls ran for the library.

"Where are we going?" Jeremy asked Leona as they bundled into their coats, boots and hats.

"To the stables," she replied. She gazed at him with her sparkling green eyes. "Do you love me, Jeremy?"

He smiled. "With all my heart, sweetness."

Leona smiled back at him. "Then you won't mind when I do this."

She leaned over and bit him on the wrist, her sharp canine teeth digging into his flesh.

Marie and Marguerite paused when they heard Jeremy scream; then they laughed and proceeded into the library.

Pale light filled the big room as completely as the musty smell of books that were never opened. A marble bust of the Corsican Butcher sat upon a nearby table and the twins kissed it. His passage through Europe provided their family a fortune, pillaging the bodies of the two-legged cattle that died in his wake. Some said the Butcher was one of the dogs that covered the battlefield like flies on a corpse, but true dogs knew better. They loved him anyway.

They looked at the pelts stretched across the wall nearest the table. Some were centuries old, collected by their ancestors from around the world. Asian giants and African pygmies, a French noble who'd wandered too far from the chateau, a Russian monk who had six fingers on each hand. Their favorite was the mad Englishman from Whitechapel; Uncle Renard himself had to put him down before he cast suspicion on several family members who lived nearby.

Moonlight filtered through the eastern window, its clean white beams pouring onto the box seat beneath the sill. The twins jumped atop the plump velvet cushions and gazed out at the night. Our Lady, serene and smiling, floated behind a gauzy white curtain of silver light, which reflected off the snow on the ground. They would have no trouble watching the fun.

For the briefest moment, they saw Grandmama, hugging her silver hair tight against her body, run past the window. Her bare feet trod lightly upon the rock salt that sparkled across the shoveled walk. White steam poured from her hot red mouth.

"Grandmama looks hungry," Marguerite observed.

Marie nodded. "But she'll wait if there is sport to be

had."

Jeremy sat groggily upon a bench in the stable and regarded the terrified man, trussed up like a turkey, in the stall in front of him. The man's dark eyes pleaded with him, but Jeremy didn't care. His bandaged wrist hurt like hell.

"I'm so sorry, dearest," Leona said from her seat beside Jeremy. "My family doesn't like long engagements."

"So, I'm a werewolf now?"

Leona shook her head and frowned. "Absolutely not. We are a proud family of dog-men, creatures who served many rulers of France for centuries. We evolved along with humans. When the monarchy withered, we came to this country, to this state before it was a state. When civilization encroached, we stayed."

Jeremy remembered reading several articles about dog-man sightings throughout the years, but he thought them nothing more than tall tales propagated as April Fool's jokes.

"Not a hoax?" he asked. "I remember that movie they found in an attic."

Leona smiled and patted his left arm.

"That was quite real. Anyway, all the dog-men you've read about are the males of our families; they truly are half-man, half-dog whenever they decide to hunt. The females can transform completely into canines; I guess you can say we are the deadlier of the species."

Jeremy regarded the blood-soaked bandage on his wrist and had to agree.

In the near distance, a rifle shot snapped through the air. Marguerite and Marie wriggled in anticipation.

"I *hate* waiting," Marguerite whispered to her sister.

"I *love* waiting," Marie murmured. "It makes the hunt even more exciting."

After several minutes, a tall man came flopping past the window as quickly as the snow and his heavy boots would allow. His eyes rolled in their sockets; white vapor gushed from his mouth as he gasped for air. Then he was gone.

"He's heading for the gate," Marguerite said, pouting. "They always do that. How boring."

"Next year will be different," Marie promised her. "We'll ask Uncle Renard to find us a hunter or soldier, somebody who'll fight."

Knowing that their relatives would have given the man a five-minute head start, they watched for Grandmama. Sure enough, she broke through the holly bushes near the pond, her long legs punching through the snow crust. Her black coat gleamed, her eyes glinted greenly, white teeth flashed in her open mouth. She shimmered across the snow and was gone.

"Shall we be as beautiful as Grandmama?" Marguerite asked.

"Oh yes," Marie said, then grabbed her arm. "Look! Here come the others!"

The sleigh lumbered into view. The girls' parents, Leona and Jeremy, and any others who chose to remain human, sat inside it. Uncle Renard stood up and shot his rifle again. Those who pulled the sleigh ran faster, their clawed feet kicking the snow into glittering clouds.

They saw the twins watching from the window and swung closer. The dog-men howled, their snouts lifted to the sky, furry breasts heaving. Uncle Renard fired the rifle a third time, and they headed off after Grandmama.

Marguerite and Marie applauded this splendid spectacle. They looked forward to it every year, and to the great feast that followed.

But that wouldn't happen for a little while yet. Marguerite and Marie passed the time by speaking of the future. They talked and watched the long hair, drawn by Our Lady's pale fingers, flow across their arms and legs.

As expected, the final scream came from the direction of the great gate, signaling the end of the Holiday Hunt. Marguerite and Marie smiled at each other, then went to retrieve their coats.

"I don't think Jeremy will join us this year," Marguerite said. "The new ones never do."

Her sister grinned as she pulled on her gloves. "More for us, dear sister. More for us."

The Invisible Beast

Zach Finn

Jean Chastel stood above the body of the strangest creature he'd ever seen in his life. The heaving animal (that was now in its death throes) had been responsible for over a hundred attacks and violent deaths in the last three years; now, it lay mortally wounded as the other hunters began to emerge from the woods to have a look. Even with all these other shooters, Chastel had clearly made the kill shot, and all the others stared at him with looks ranging from awe to jealously. He had, after all, braved the open field (which left him completely vulnerable to the beast's charge) in order to have a clear line of sight. Although the monster had seemed invulnerable to bullets up until that point, Chattel's shot rang true, and the creature had crumpled into a heap mid-rush. The giant, copper colored monster snarled one last time as if in defiance of its killer, before it's muscular body slackened and its head fell to the ground. The Beast of Gevaudan was finally dead, and the people of the Margeride

Mountains in France could now rest easy, knowing that their arch nemesis was no more.....

This was definitely Buster's best walk ever. Sure the plane flight over had been far from his favorite thing; sitting in a crate stuffed into the bottom of an airplane traversing the Atlantic Ocean would be rough for anyone (and it had been especially rough for the hyperactive boxer-Pit bull Terrier mix), but now, the rigors of the flight were as far from his mind as he and his owner were from their American apartment as they backpacked the French mountain range of the Margeride Mountains.

Unbeknown to Buster, he had almost not been allowed into France because of his breed and the strict restrictions put on pit bull's specifically. Luckily for him though, his owner had anticipated the issues they might run into getting to the country, and he had planned accordingly. It also helped that Buster's appearance looked slightly more Boxer'ish than like a stereotypical American Pit bull: He was a stark black, apart from white patches that ran from his belly, over his neck, and down the center of his face. He was also a little guy, who only weighed about thirty five pounds soaking wet. So after a brief explanation to airport workers, who thought all pit bulls were giants (and also with the the help of a friendly vet back home who had changed his listing from "American Staffordshire Terrier/Boxer mix" to "Boxer mix" on his travel papers) Buster was allowed into France to accompany his owner on their hike through the beautiful Margeride Mountains.

They had been walking for about three days now, and had seen the Truyere river, the beautiful fields and meadows of the region, and the Allier Valley; and they were now resting in the city of Sauges catching their breath and grabbing some much needed refreshments after the strenuous few days.

As Buster and his owner rested at a local coffee shop, Buster lay on his side soaking in the sun that splashed down on the outside pavilion they now rested, having taken his full from the portable water bowl that sat nearly empty before him. His owner meanwhile, was drinking a sweet local coffee drink which he hoped would give him some energy to continue on their trek. As the two sat, people watching and catching their breath, a local show began to unfold in the streets, drawing in tourists with its colorful display and charismatic actors.

The commotion caused Buster to stir from his half-nap, and he sat up, taking in the chaos that was going on in front of him. What the particular story was escaped the young dog; but he could make out the rough outline of a giant red dog (or animal?), that was attacking the humans in the play. Buster let out a guttural growl when the commotion got a little to realistic.

"Quiet Bud" his owner whispered, as he leaned forward to rub underneath Buster's chin in an effort to calm the dog down. Having his chin rubbed was Buster's favorite thing in the world (next to peanut butter), and his initial fears of whatever the monster in the play was began to die down, and his eyes closed slowly, and eventually he returned to sunbathing on the warm pavement.

Buster's owner was, as it stood, completely entrenched in the story unfolding before his eyes. The narrator of the play, a tall skinny man who was dressed in period appropriate attire, told of the Beast of Gevaudan, an animal who had brutally murdered folks throughout the mountains they were walking by ripping out their throats, and-if hungry- partially devouring the corpse of the victim, leaving behind grotesque scenes of violence for whoever stumbled upon the remains. The beast remained at large for a while, and even when a large wolf like creature that many believed to be the monster was killed, the killings continued for another year or so. It wasn't until the hero of the story Chastel (who was played by what appeared to be a bodybuilder, and was introduced with much applause) fired that fateful shot that the people of the region could rest easy, no longer terrified of the giant monster that prowled their hills.

Buster began to stir again as the clapping commenced, but he eventually became distracted with a rubber chew toy his owner had thought to pull out of his oversized hiking pack so he could enjoy the rest of the play.

The narrator concluded the performance listing the various theories of what the beast may have been-and there were a lot of them. Some theorized that the beast was a single wolf, or perhaps a wolf pack. Others believed it was a lion that had escaped a traveling circus. And others still believed it was something stranger-perhaps a previously unnamed cryptid animal or a werewolf. Whatever the beast was, it now served as a critical element of the tourist industry for the town. So much so, in fact, the town even had a local museum dedicated to the beast.

After the play ended and the crowds dispersed, Buster's owner stood up, stretched out his arms, shouldered his hiking pack, and untied Buster's leash from the chair he had been anchored to and the two began to walk through the town. As they walked through the cobbled streets, admiring the stores, smelling the delicious smells, and enjoying the local flare, the beast from the play earlier skitted briefly across both of their memories, likely influenced by the various touristy attractions that displayed the local legend.

Those thoughts only lasted briefly though; Buster's focus soon became engaged on the smell of the local delicacies floating through the air, while his owner was distracted by the pretty local girls who strolled by. As they made their way out of town, thoughts of the monster that had roamed the hills hundreds of years ago barely registered, and the excitement of the adventure overtook them.

They hiked the gorgeous hills, all the while walking past ancient ancestral homes, houses whose previous owners had lived in fear of the monster that's attacks had been so vicious, they often left the victim's headless after the monster was done with them. But all this was unknown to the two travelers.

Not much had changed in the rural outskirts of the area since those days, and as they walked the two felt transported back to another time, a time when the woods and nature were more than scary: they were unknown and evil-housing devils, witches, and creatures. A time when the French peasants had locked their doors, afraid that the beast ripping out the throats of their friends might be more than just a rogue wolf.

But despite these underlying feelings of uneasiness, they were both enjoying the scenic moors and lakes of the area. They walked for what felt like forever (about 10 kilometers) before they decided to make camp for the night. Since he brought Buster, his owner had decided to bring a small, light tent as opposed to trying his luck at hostels that may or may not be dog friendly.

They had a good routine for camp set up. First, they would find an uninhabited plot of land; far enough from the road where they wouldn't be seen, but close enough to where they could find it in the dark need be. As Buster's owner sat down and plotted where the tent would go, Buster scampered around their makeshift campsite alternating his attention between chasing a butterfly that had floated past, and chewing a stick that demanded his attention.

As Buster gnawed on the stick, he began to notice a smell that permeated the air. His nose stuck up attempting to access whatever the odor was that was being carried across the wind, and he quickly inhaled in rapid succession to try and decipher what it might be.

While he couldn't place it specifically, the smell registered to Buster on a primal level, similar to how some humans are afraid of the water, or of heights. The hatred of that smell was as much an inherent part of him as his eyes, and nose, and the birthmark on his stomach were, and it was coded down so deep in his DNA that he could not exist without the aversion to the smell being a part of him. All animals have it; it runs deeper than anything science can measure, and perhaps it explains why some animals still walk the earth, while others died out.

And while the smell sparked warning signs that Buster might not understand completely; he understood what they meant. It meant to run. And run far, far away. It was a warning system that had its origins in times when humans and dogs were barely connected. When the woods, especially at night, was a dark blanket of impenetrable depth only broken by the gleaming pinpoints of light, reflecting off the eyes of creatures adept at killing, and killing well. It said something was coming and this something had bad intentions.

Once it registered, Buster shot up with a shrill yip, that startled his owner into dropping the pan he was carrying as he attempted to prepare their dinner meal.

"Shhhhhh…." his owner said soothingly to him, hoping that Buster's noises wouldn't attract company. He honestly had no idea if he was trespassing or not, and as friendly as the towns they were passing through seemed, he didn't want to get caught out here alone by some drunk locals or something like that. He had heard enough horror stories to know that travelers were especially tempting targets for thieves and pickpockets, especially when they were camping by themselves in the woods with no one around.

Despite his owners prodding, Buster was continuing to make a scene. Howling (a sound that his owner had never heard him do), kicking up leaves, and scampering around the tree he was tied to. In the same way Buster's actions were confusing his owner, Buster was just as flustered by his owners behavior: he couldn't believe his owner wasn't freaking out. How in God's name could he not be packing up his bags and making a run for it? Didn't he know this wasn't safe?

A howl pierced the air. Buster stopped moving. His eyes jetted around, attempting to find the source of whatever creature produced the haunting sound. When he couldn't locate it, his glances shot to his owner, who was carrying on like he hadn't heard a thing. It was like how when Buster heard thunder coming from far away, yet his owner sat completely unaware to the sound as Buster bounded around their apartment attempting to find somewhere to take cover.

The howl split the night again; this time, is sounded louder, more agitated; like an animal caught in a trap screaming for vengeance. It didn't stop at one howl, the screeches continued for what felt like an eternity.

But still, nothing from his owner, who had given up on the meal in the pan and sat snacking on one of those military meals they sell at sport stores for hikers, talking half to himself, and half to Buster.

"We should try and make it into another town tomorrow boy."

By this point, Buster had given up howling and had switched to pacing and listening for whatever was making the noises he was hearing, sounds that were getting progressively closer to their makeshift campsite. The fight or flight adrenaline rush surged over Buster, and, seeing as he was anchored to a tree, he was forced to choose the latter. He stopped pacing, and stood silently, ready for an attack from any angle. His weight shifted forward, lowering and protecting his neck from whatever was making its way to the treeline. The howls had subsided to growls, deep, rumbling growls that practically shook the earth. Buster bared his teeth, forgetting his oblivious owner had no idea what was coming.

"Buster!" his owner yelled, "What's gotten into you tonight?"

The sudden aggression in Buster, his owner assumed, was probably due to the stressful couple of days the young dog had undergone. Hell, he still hadn't recovered from the jet lag, and this was far from his first trip abroad. Buster must have been feeling even worse.

In the same way that he had prepared for getting Buster through customs, Buster's owner had also prepared for something like this to happen. He had packed some anti-anxiety medicine from the vet, which would likely knock Buster out for the next couple of hours. While he wasn't a fan of his guard dog being asleep, it seemed like the best choice at this time.

"Come here bud, it's been a rough couple of days, hasn't it?" he said, scooping out Buster's favorite treat (a spoonful of peanut butter) from its packaging and dropping the small, pink tablet gracefully on the mound that rested on the spoon.

Even in his worked up state, Buster's eyes still lit up when he saw the peanut butter. The same ancestral coding that made Buster resent that smell, also made him love treats; and, since the growling had temporarily subsided, the young dog decided a quick break from his duty (plus a reward) was well earned. As his owner made his way over to the tree, Buster pranced forward excitedly, and gobbled up the peanut butter in record time.

The medicine hit almost immediately. As he made his way back towards the tree, his pace began to slow. He was about five feet from his resting spot when the growls resumed. Buster gave it his all to howl, to warn his owner, anything, but his body felt like it was shutting down. He had never been this tired before, not even when he was a puppy and his owner brought him swimming for the first time and the cold water had sapped his energy...but that was nothing compared to this. He turned towards his owner, and began walking closer to him-he had to warn him. His owner, for his part, was setting up his tent and sleeping bag close enough for Buster to reach him. He also slept with the tent's entrance flap wide open, so Buster could come and go as he pleased, while still being anchored to something outside.

Each step felt like a mile. Buster was almost there. Ten feet. Five feet. He was going to make it, to warn his owner. Behind him, the growls were coming from much closer than they had before. Whatever was making them sounded like it was almost by the tree Buster was tied to. It didn't matter, he was almost there to protect him…the last thing Buster heard before he crashed into a sea of unconscious dreams was his owners chuckle, saying "man that stuff works fast", and a howl coming from right behind them…

Buster woke suddenly at around 3 am. He had been asleep for 5 hours straight, and his dreams had been filled with primordial monsters attacking his owner while, and no matter how fast he ran, he couldn't catch up with them to save him. He looked around and in a split second, the young dog was able to gather the information that: A) somehow he ended up in the tent, B) his owner was right next to him, and was sleeping soundly, and C) the smell was still there, and whatever was making it was sitting right behind the tree he was tied too.

The earlier dread Buster had felt was subsided. Perhaps it was the horrible dreams he had just experienced, or maybe the fear was just dulled since he had already been exposed to it; whatever it was, Buster rushed out to greet the nameless monster immediately.

As he rushed out, the creature stepped out from behind the tree, and it's massive frame suddenly came into view for the first time. It was giant, weighing in at around 200 pounds and standing at least five feet from front paw to head. It could have been mistaken for a calf from a distance. Up close though, any mistaken identity would have been removed. Sharp teeth protruded from its grimace and filled its mouth with flesh tearing, bone crunching, fangs that seemed to glisten in the night. It's eyes reflected the light of the moon, and practically illuminated the rest of its ferocious face. Although Buster couldn't tell due to being color blind, the coloring of the animal was a mix of copper red and steely gray, that gave it the appearance of a wolf-lion hybrid. It's long tail sat straight up as well, ready to attack.   Buster ran towards the beast, barking ferociously. The normally friendly (and while far from perfectly behaved) good dog looked like something out of a nightmare. His jet black fur blended into the night, with only his teeth (which were certainly intimidating) and the small patch of white on his forehead giving any show that he was coming forward. He stopped his frantic charge about five feet from the Beast of Gevaudan, slowing to a measured pace. His teeth flashed, and a haunting growl emitted from somewhere much deeper than any physical organ in his body could produce. The growl from Buster traced its origin to a time when dogs and humans made their first pact to protect each other as they forged their way through terra incognito.

The beast took a step back. It had expected easy human prey, not this. Ever the apex predator, it began to devise its next move.

At the same time, Buster's owner emerged from the tent, having been woken by Buster's bark. In his hand was the grey spray bottle he carried with him to squirt Buster when he was being bad (a tip he had borrowed from his parents, who had two giant, well-behaved pits).

"Buster, what the hell are you doing?" he hollered, spritzing Buster with a jet of water.

Buster was too worked up to care. He simply stood chest to the ground, growling at the monster.

"Come back in the tent bud" his owner, said oblivious to the beast Buster kept at bay.

Even at his young age, Buster knew there were some things dogs could see that humans couldn't; and the giant monster was one of those things.

Buster's owner went to pull the trigger on the bottle again, and for the first time, the (ghost of the) Beast of Gevaudan broke his gaze from Buster, and lifted it to Buster's owner.

Perhaps the bottle reminded him of one of the many

handguns that had shot him during his reign of terror, or perhaps, being outnumbered, the monster decided it wasn't worth it. Whatever the reason, the beast that only Buster could see began to slowly slink back into the woods. When he disappeared from sight, and eventually scent, Buster sat up. He was back to his usual self.

"You're a freaking nut today bud" his owner said, lovingly petting his head as Buster trotted up to him, victorious in a battle the owner couldn't even begin to appreciate. The two headed for the tent, and plopped down tired, from their travels, adventures, and (for one of them), a battle of will against the ghost of a notorious cryptid monster.

Somewhere far, far away, a howl whispered through the night.

"I bet you it's that beast of Gevaudan…..Javeedee……. Gevaudan, or however you say it" his owner jokingly told Buster, scratching his ears as he cuddled up next to him on the sleeping bag.

But the joke fell on deaf ears, as the medicine and toils of the day took their toll on the young dog, who was fast asleep.

Buster had more dreams like he did earlier, dreams of monsters in the darkness and his owner; but this time, he caught up to his them, saved his owner, and got rewarded with peanut butter. Buster's owner was woken up throughout the night to the sound of Buster's tail stirring in his sleep, wagging happily as he cuddled closer to his chuckling owner, who was glad he brought the young dog along.

Many Winters

Samantha Rich

This is the river; this is the shore. Before — *before* —
there were trees, here, yes, it was thick with trees, bushes, grasses
grew tall, the people sometimes burned them, enough that the
next season they would burn again. In the winter the snow fell
thick-fast-deep, but the trees held it back, broke it into pieces,
there was room to move among, and the river froze heavy-solid,
the wind could sweep it clear.

One the open river he would *run* and *run* and *run*,
feel the wind, sing to the earth, sunlight touching skin but not
enough to warm it. And the people saw him from the shore, they
gestured, they said his name in old words, they called him a spirit
of the land and the river, and he came back to the shore, and he
danced.

It was. Things *were*. That was before.

He felt himself change, when the other-people came, the
ones who didn't call themselves *the people*, but other words for
the self and the group, and the threads of self and group ran over

the land to somewhere far away, over places he didn't understand and water that was too wide and deep to sing.

He was made of stories, shaped by the words of the people; what they said he was, they made him. The new-people, the other-people, they had their own stories, their own words, and their stories blended with the people's stories, on the banks of the river, on the shore, and they built a new place there. It reshaped the shore; the words reshaped him, just a little, cut here, build there.

His face went red and his teeth rotten, a wide grin across the wizened skin and human skull, while his body still worked on two feet or four-in-a-hurry, and his fur stayed heavy and matted to keep him warm.

He danced on the shore, and the people still knew him, they called him a spirit of the land and the river.

The other-people saw him only out of the corners of their eyes, and they made sounds of horror, and in their other-tongue, their *French*, they called him *Le Nain Rouge*.

He understood the French better, the longer they stayed. They built and built, cut back the trees, burned the grasses, changed the edges of the river. It still ran fast, in summer, and froze smooth, in winter, but the edges were changed, crowded with boats that got bigger and bigger. He danced, and they cried out, and threw things at him. Rocks, garbage-things, fire-things.

The people left, in time, he didn't see them anymore, still felt them in the earth and the water, still heard them along the shore, through his feet, when he danced. He remembered what the part of him was, from *before*, that part that blended into Le Nain Rouge, with its old old job to do.

Watch the land, dance, run the river, taste danger and doom on the wind and warn whoever would listen. He didn't speak their words, he never had, but his face was warning enough, see his face and his body, see him run the street and dance in the air. They should know. They knew before. Now they cried out in their French, and threw rocks, and he kept running.

Let them know or not-know. He knew. That had always been his, to know, to taste on the wind and *know*, if they listened or not, he knew.

The man in the night—the man with the stick, who struck out and knocked him back—Le Nain Rouge didn't *know* him. Men were not what he knew, he knew the words that made him, the river and the shore, the taste of danger-doom-trouble, the feel of ice and earth under his feet when he danced.

The man — *Cadillac*, the other-people called him, *de la*

Mothe Cadillac — struck him and he ran away, leaving the shore and the river for the sky and disappearing into the night.

The troubles that followed were not *from* him, he didn't bring them, oh no, that was not his task. He only tasted and knew, he only came and warned with his body, his face, his dance.

They called it war, they called it *Bloody Run*, the little river ran thick-red with bodies spilling blood, it carried down the way to the true river, his river. It was summer, air heavy with heat, no ice on the water. He danced on the shore instead, danced among the bodies.

He had danced before the war, too, for the people and the other-people, both saw him, he warned them both that this would come, this trouble, this thick salt blood on the shore and in the water, this fire and bullets, this pain.

Cadillac was gone, but the people's leader, *Pontiac*, he saw Le Nain Rouge, and knew him, knew the pieces from *before* blended in with the French stories that reshaped him. *Pontiac* nodded, made a gesture of respect, and went on with what he had to do, the warning not enough, the need for war unstoppable, and the little river ran red, stopped up with corpses.

The buildings bred true and grew across the land, so

many, *la cité* they called it, and *Detroit*, French words, they shaped the city and the land, they shaped him more. He had hands now, he could grab and climb, it was an interesting change.

Detroit bred and grew, Le Nain Rouge tasted on the wind that it would burn, and he ran through its streets, letting himself be seen, telling them with his face and his body and his dance that danger came behind him.

He did not *start* the fires, he did not *bring* the fires, he only *warned*, but they didn't know the difference, they cursed his name and shook their fists.

I saw Le Nain Rouge, they said. I *saw him before the fires. He did this.*

I saw him too! He's a monster. A demon. He brings death on his heels—didn't they see him before the Battle of Bloody Run? Didn't the fortune teller warn de la Mothe Cadillac that the sight of Le Nain Rouge brought trouble and despair?

He danced on the air, on the shore, among the remaining trees. Heavy warm summer again, no ice, and the river too thick with boats for him to dance there.

Detroit was still burning, its people still shouting and cursing in the ash and heat. They blamed him, they blamed him, and he danced. He had no words to tell them that he brought nothing, he only tasted the warnings and ran. He had never been made for words, he didn't need them, after all.

Time passed and passed. The river changed. The city changed. The streets grew black and scaly, heavy warm tar. It felt good under his feet, when he ran, when he danced.

In the winter, the snow piled high high high, no trees to break it into pieces. He climbed over it, scrambled onto the drifts to look through windows and into the lights they hung on poles. First the lights held fire, bright dancing, what he understood, and he warmed his hands on them. Then the lights glowed but there was no fire, only layers of glass, and they warmed his hands a little but not as much.

The river grew thick and ugly, water too heavy with muck to sparkle in the sun. But it still froze in winter, and when the boats rested in the cold there was enough room to dance.

There was a bridge now, to the other side where he didn't go, because it had never been his piece of land and river and shore. Something else had lived over there, he didn't know if it lingered or not, it didn't matter. Metal beasts, big ones, ran back and forth, over the bridge, through the streets of the city. He chased them, when he wanted; he danced atop them, when they slept.

Sometimes he tasted on the wind that deep snow would come; sometimes that a storm would come and wipe out the wires the city now used to live. He didn't know their purpose, but he knew the taste of danger, and like he always had, he went to tell them, these people who lived on his bit of land and river and shore.

They screamed when they saw him, sometimes they shot bullets, but he ran ran ran, through the streets, over the rooftops. This was his and he would do as he had always done.

They kept changing, these people. Their words changed, their thoughts changed. He changed in return, as he always had, reshaped by them, made new, made different.

These words made him thinner-smaller-faded. They thought in larger pieces, straighter lines, and so did he, because they shaped him.

He still tasted danger and ran to show them, but some of them couldn't see him anymore. Most of them, maybe, it was hard to tell. Eyes looked past him or through him. Sometimes they squinted, cocked their heads, like they thought *maybe* they saw something, a piece, a ghost, but...

It didn't matter so much. It was his job to warn, it was

theirs to listen, or not. Faded and thin but not gone, he could still run, still dance.

There were empty buildings, burned-out spaces, fallen things. There were places where the forest ghost was trying to break back through the ground, growing up in grass brush flowers. The river ran cleaner, it sparkled in the sun, now. The ice was thinner in winter, the cold not so deep, but the snow still came, and piled thick where it could.

There were fewer people in some places, more in others. Some still saw him. Some still screamed, others stared in wonder. Whatever came next, following at his heels, they coped with it, found their way around it, endured.

This is the river, this is the shore, this is the city. Its body and bones stand over the land-that-is-his, where he tastes the wind and runs up and down the things they put before him, where he dances on the air and on the shore, and has forever, and will forever. He changes with the times and the thoughts and the people who live here, but he is *here*, and will be, before and after.

The city falls and rises, the land ebbs and builds at the river edge, and he is here.

Picnicking with Old Yellow Top

Adam Millard

I

Cobalt, Ontario, 19—

It was an unseasonably warm day and the Deshane family had spent much of the morning bickering about whether to forge ahead with their plans to head on out to the Wettlaufer mines for a spot to eat. Ethan Deshane, while working up at the mine on the north side, had stumbled upon a wonderful location—a perfect mixture of trail and lake—and wanted his family to see it, to experience its splendour, before summer was over.

"We'll stick to the shade," he'd assured his family that morning. "And we'll wear hats. The sun won't stand a chance."

After a little resistance (mainly Madison, whose raven hair and fair skin often left her at the mercy of summer) they had climbed into the family Plymouth and left Haileybury shortly after ten.

Johnny, sitting in the back with his toy soldiers, looked up only when he had a question to ask; at twelve years old, Johnny had a lot of questions. "Do you think we'll see any wolves up at the mine today?" he asked, shortly after their journey began. Johnny was fascinated by wolves, simply couldn't get enough of them.

"Let's hope not," replied Madison, visibly shuddering. "Horrible things."

Johnny thought about educating his wife a little, explaining how wolves were such an important part of the Ontario ecosystem, but decided against it when she shot him a reproachful glance. She must have known, must have sensed his intention, and had pre-empted it with a reproving look.

"I haven't seen a wolf up here in months," he called back to Johnny, who had been waiting on tenterhooks, leaning forward in his seat so that Ethan could feel the boy's warm breath on the nape of his neck. "More'n likely catch a glimpse of a caribou, though, if you keep your wits about you."

Johnny slumped back in his seat, seemingly dejected. "Caribous are boring, Dad," he said. "I've seen a hundred of them."

Ethan sighed. "No more questions, Johnny, okay? We'll be there shortly, and you can go off a-hunting for wolves, if that's what you want to do."

"Don't tell him that, Ethan," Madison said, her voice tinged with annoyance. To Johnny in the back, she said, "Ignore your father, Johnny. There will be no wolf-hunts today, or any other day, for that matter." She turned back to the front and exhaled loudly. "Damned things'll eat you up before you get a chance to scream for help."

Ethan glanced into the rear-view mirror, saw Johnny's face illuminate with the possibilities. His son was fearless. Stupid, but fearless. Just like Ethan had been at the same age. Ethan loved his son more than anything in the world, wanted what was best for him—hoped he would not end up at the Cobalt Lode in the next few years, searching for silver that, most of the time, wasn't there—and striving each day to do what was best by him. Being a father was not easy, but Ethan wouldn't have it any other way.

"How much farther, Dad?" Johnny had taken to impatiently tapping on the window, and Ethan had been about to censure him when the question came.

"Couple of miles," Ethan said. "Give or take. We can't get all the way up to the spot in the car, but I figure we'll have less'n a mile to walk."

"You never mentioned anything about hiking!" Madison said, her eyes and mouth comically wide in the passenger seat. "Ethan Deshane, I do believe this picnic is the worst idea you have ever had in all the years we've been together."

"It's just a little hike, is all," Ethan said. "And besides, it's good to work up an appetite." The amount of food his wife had prepared that morning was enough to feed a small army.

"And what if something goes wrong?" Madison asked, all at once very serious indeed. "What if… what if something happens to one of us while we're up there—"

"Like what?" Ethan interrupted.

"Like, I don't know… what if Johnny turns his ankle. That mile to the car is going to seem like ten if you have to carry him."

Ethan shook his head. "Nothing's going to happen up there, Madison," he said, for nothing ever did. He had worked up at those mines for long enough to know the terrain. If Johnny turned his ankle, it would be his own stupid fault. "Like I said, I haven't seen a wolf in months. Unless…" He trailed off there for dramatic effect, knowing it would elicit a series of questions from both his wife and son.

"Unless what?" Madison said.

"Unless…?" said Johnny, leaning forward in his seat once again, his eyes wide.

Ethan shrugged. "Well, I guess everyone in town will know about it soon enough," he said, for he was an expert in building suspense, loved to tell stories down in the mine to anyone who would listen. Besides, the story he was about to tell was true, at least some elements of it. It was just a case of upping the ante.

"You remember Burt McCarthy?" The question was aimed at Madison; Johnny wouldn't know Burt from Adam.

"The barber?" Madison said, and when Ethan nodded, she added, "What about him?"

Ethan knew this would have to be good. A yarn with all the trimmings, lest his wife shut him down before he'd even begun. And where was the fun in that?

"Well, according to Sid Paulson, Burt was out walking along the north side of the Cobalt Lode with his dog when he stopped to tamp his pipe. Cassie, that's the name of his dog, slipped her lead and off she went. Burt's not getting any younger, and so it was all he could do to keep up."

"I saw Burt just yesterday," Madison said, "so if he dies in this story, I'll know it's nonsense."

"I didn't say anything about him dying," Ethan replied. "No, what happened to Burt McCarthy is much, much worse."

"What happened to Burt, Dad?" Johnny called excitedly from the back.

"Well, Burt chased little Cassie as best he could. Wound up down by the lake. You see, Cassie loves the water, and she was in there quicker'n you can say abracadabra." He paused for dramatic effect. "Burt was calling to her to get out of the lake when… something moved in the trees to his right."

"Was it wolves, Dad?" Johnny's excitement was palpable.

Ethan shook his head. "Burt would have taken wolves over what he saw. According to Sid Paulson, Burt saw a monster step out of those trees. At least seven feet tall. A hulking beast of a creature, with a long flowing mane of golden hair."

In the passenger seat, Madison clicked her tongue. "Burt wouldn't happen to have been drinking that rancid moonshine he makes in the backroom of his barbershop," she said, her tone drenched with derision. "Long flowing mane of golden hair… really?"

"That's what he told Sid Paulson," Ethan said. "Cassie must have seen it, too. She jumped out of the lake and ran for the hills. Burt wasn't too far behind her. Said the monster went back into the trees, roaring and beating its chest like something out of a nightmare."

Johnny relaxed back in his seat. "I hope we see it," he said, smiling.

Madison looked over to Ethan, whose work here was done. "You see?" she said. "Filling the boy's head with tales of monsters and things that should not be?"

Things that should not be?

Ethan liked than analogy.

When they pulled up at the foot of the Cobalt Lode a few minutes later, he was still rolling the words around his mouth, as if they were the best damn thing he had ever tasted.

II

The hike up to the picnic spot was unbearable, and by the time they arrived, Ethan was coated in a thin film of sweat and his palms were sore from carrying the wicker hamper. He didn't complain once, though, since this whole thing had been his idea; the last thing he wanted was to give Madison the ammunition to tell him 'Told you so!'.

"What do you think?" Ethan said, motioning to their surroundings. "The lake is just down there, and you see that trail over yonder? That goes all the way back to the Cobalt Lode. That was how I found this place. I don't think many people know about it, and I'd like to keep it that way for as long as possible."

Madison laid out a large blanket and began unpacking food from the hamper. "It's a nice spot," she ceded. "Not sure it was worth the hike up here, but I'm not going to complain."

Ethan watched as the picnic began to take shape. There were savouries of all kinds, and cakes which Madison had spent the previous evening baking. By the time everything was in place, Ethan's stomach was growling so hard, you would have thought there were wolves in the area.

"Dad, can we go take a look at the lake?" Johnny was yet to sit on the blanket; he had spent the last ten minutes pacing up and down the hill, eager to explore.

"After we eat," Ethan told him, to which Johnny responded with a frustrated sigh. "Sit down, son. Your mother's gone to a lot of trouble with all this food. And you're gonna want to get some of it inside you. What if you have to run away from the giant with the golden mane, huh? You don't have any food in you, you won't get far before the beast catches up to you. And then..." He rushed across the clearing and wrestled Johnny to the ground, biting and tickling the boy until he was in fits of uncontrollable laughter. Ethan loved to hear it; his boy meant everything to him.

"When you two are quite finished," Madison said as she carved at a seeded loaf, "the picnic's ready."

Ethan released Johnny, helped him to his feet before brushing dead grass away from his clothing. "You heard your mother," he said. "Go get some grub."

They ate heartily, a veritable feast of buttermilk fried chicken, devilled eggs, grilled ham and Swiss sandwiches, potato salad, crackers, peppered tomatoes, all washed down with homemade lemonade. Ethan told more stories as the food went down, and Johnny listened raptly, blissfully absorbed by his father's tales and, for once, seemingly without questions. Madison gazed wistfully at all around her, occasionally nibbling on a devilled egg, but for the most part she sat smiling at the scenery.

"Can we go see the lake now?" Johnny asked, setting his plate down on the blanket. The question was aimed at Ethan, rather than Madison, for Johnny knew the final decision would be made by his father.

Though not until Ethan gained approval from Madison with a sideward glance.

"Don't be gone too long," Madison said, flicking an insect from her leg. "I'm not packing all this stuff away on my lonesome."

Johnny excitedly punched the air as Ethan climbed languorously to his feet. He had eaten far too much, and would have preferred to sit for a while, let it all go down before accompanying Johnny down to the lake. Still, he was up now. Might as well enjoy the wilderness while it lasted. Tomorrow he would be back at the mine, sweltering and filthy and surrounded by uncouth fools.

Moments like these should be cherished so that he might call upon the memories whilst down in the claustrophobic darkness.

They slowly descended the hill. Johnny stopped occasionally to wave at his mother, and Madison waved back. She was already packing the food away, and Ethan felt all at once guilty.

"Be careful," he called out to Johnny, who was getting too far ahead for his liking. "You'll turn your ankle." And wouldn't Madison just love that? 'Told you so!' she would say as Ethan carried their son to the Plymouth. 'I just knew he would turn his ankle.' And an argument would ensue, all the way to the hospital with an undigested picnic sitting uncomfortably in Ethan's stomach.

Fortunately, Johnny paid heed to Ethan and slowed to a jaunty skip.

They slipped into the treeline, and it was there that the lake could be heard, its waters gently splashing back and forth over rocks.

"Stay by my side," Ethan said, helping his son over a fallen tree. Although there had been no sightings of wolves in recent weeks, here in the woods there could be plenty, using the canopy as shade from the overbearing sun above.

"This is swell!" Johnny said, reaching down to pick up

a stick from the undergrowth. He swung it through the air—whiiiiiish—and rejoiced at the sound it made. Such innocence, Ethan thought. Such an anticipation for life. He envied the boy, for his own enthusiasm for the simple things, which had once enchanted him so, had begun to inexorably fade. Would it ever return? Was losing that lust for life just something every adult human experienced as time wore on?

They arrived at the lake just a few minutes after entering the woods, and stood there, father and son, fixated upon the water and the sunlight dancing across it. Neither spoke straight away, but it was only a matter of time before Johnny's first question, and Ethan silently waited until his son was ready to ask it.

"Are we allowed to fish here?" Johnny looked up at Ethan with hope in his eyes.

"I don't see why not," Ethan said. "I mean, whether it's legal, that's another thing entirely, but we could always bring our gear up here and make an afternoon of it."

"Mom wouldn't let me," Johnny said, somewhat dejected.

"Who says she has to know?" Ethan replied, winking at the boy and eliciting an instant mischievous grin. Ethan turned his attention back to the sprawling waters in front of them, and found himself pondering the types of fish beneath its surface.

Walleye? Northern pike? Muskie or Smallmouth bass? There could be all kinds of fish in there, each as tasty as the next. Yes, a fishing trip with Johnny was most definitely on the cards in the coming weeks. And besides, it gave them both something to look forward to, some much-needed father and son time. Ethan spent so much time in Cobalt Lode that he'd neglected his duties as a father, eschewed them even in order to put food on the table.

"Five more minutes and we'll have to get back," Ethan said. He was already starting to worry about leaving Madison all alone.

"Okay, Dad," Johnny said through a disappointed sigh.

"Hey!" Ethan nudged his son in the ribs. "Think about your poor mother for a change. Think about how guilty you'd feel if she was gobbled up by wolves while we were down here staring at the lake."

Johnny laughed. "I would feel guilty," he said. "But as the minor here, the onus would fall on you."

"And as the miner here," Ethan said, feeling proud of his improvised wordplay, "I think we should get back now, before it's too late." He ruffled Johnny's hair and turned away from the water, and it was then that he saw something shifting through the trees in front of them. Johnny, who hadn't noticed the movement, was about to skip off in the direction from whence they had come when Ethan latched onto his shoulder, stopping him in his tracks.

"Don't move," Ethan whispered. Johnny looked up at Ethan with so many questions on his quivering lips. Ethan simply shook his head and kept his eyes fixed on the woods in front. There had been something there a moment ago, he was certain of it. Something large. A bear, perhaps, although the last bear Ethan had seen was over in Devil's Rock almost two years ago, and there had been no reports of bear sightings in the vicinity of Cobalt Lode for as long as he could remember.

Johnny squeezed Ethan's hand, his palm all at once clammy and hot. All that talk of encountering wolves had been bravado; Johnny was terrified and, Ethan thought, wishing he'd never said such things in jest earlier that morning.

"It's okay, son," Ethan said, keeping his voice low and steady. "Whatever it was, I think it's gone." Still, he watched the trees, making sure he was right before heading back to Madison at the top of the hill.

After a few more seconds of silence, Ethan exhaled, for he had been holding his breath without realising it.

"You were just messing with me, Dad," Johnny said. He too looked relieved. "I should have known you'd pull something like this."

Ethan was about to tell him that he was sure he had seen something in the trees when, off to their right, there came a hellish roar. Ethan's heart leapt into his throat as he snatched Johnny up from the ground and raced for the trees, away from the lake and the growling unknown.

Johnny was sobbing now in Ethan's arms, his whole body hitching with each lamenting moan. Over rocks and roots Ethan barrelled, almost slipping as the sonorous rumble of the chasing creature appeared to be right there behind them.

Ethan, still running, looked back, saw the thing in pursuit, and almost went mad in an instant.

A creature—at least seven feet tall and with a mane of golden hair—hurtled over fallen trees, its eyes fixed upon Ethan, its yellowed teeth bared in a perpetual snarl. It was just as Burt McCarthy had described it to Sid Paulson, only ten times more terrifying. How the old man had managed to outrun the thing, Ethan did not know, for it was already gaining on him, was almost upon him with its gigantic hands and fur as black as night.

"Dad!" Johnny cried.

"It's okay, son!" Ethan assured him. But it wasn't okay, for the creature was bearing down on them, and the clearing at the foot of the hill was so far ahead that Ethan knew they were not going to make it. "Close your eyes!"

Whether Johnny closed his eyes or not, Ethan would never know.

The beast thumped into his back, knocking him from his feet and sending Johnny flying from his arms and across the woods.

And when Ethan rolled to a halt he looked up, saw the rays of light seeping in through the canopy give way to darkness and rancid breath, and he knew he would not see his son again.

The creature roared once, beat its chest, and sank its teeth into the top of Ethan's head.

There was an audible pop! and then nothing else but darkness.

III

Madison placed the last few dirty plates in the hamper and closed the lid; Ethan and Johnny wouldn't be much longer, she hoped, for she wanted to get home to her garden while there was still plenty of sun to enjoy.

She walked back and forth along the crest of the hill, glancing down at the point in the trees through which her husband

and son had vanished almost an hour before. Any moment now, she thought, they would emerge. Johnny reluctantly trailing behind Ethan, disappointed that they had encountered no wolves.

Any moment now.

The sun was at its hottest, and Madison returned to the shaded picnic blanket beneath the tree. "Come on, Ethan," she muttered, once again fixing her eyes upon the woods at the foot of the hill.

No sooner had she spoke than, from the trees, came Johnny. He was running, and screaming out for her.

Madison got to her feet and frantically began to make her way down the hill, fearing the worst. Where was Ethan? What had happened to Ethan? Why was Johnny screaming like that? As if his life depended on it?

She was halfway down, and around two-hundred metres from Johnny— "No, Mom! Turn around! Run!"—when the thing emerged from the trees. Madison saw it, and it was her turn to scream, or would have been had it not caught in her throat like thick tar. Her legs suddenly stopped working, and she came to a staccato halt.

"Johnny!" she cried, for the boy was struggling to make it up the hill and the monster—it was the monster, the one Burt had seen when Cassie had slipped her leash—was almost caught up to him.

"Mom!" Johnny said, tears glistening upon his cheeks. He slowed, bounded once or twice, more to the side than anything, and then dropped to his knees, exhausted.

The Goliathan thing, with one heavy swipe of its arm, knocked Johnny's head sideways. From where she stood, Madison heard the crack, and she knew he was gone. His neck had broken, his skull had caved in. The life in her son had been extinguished as she stood watching, powerless to do anything.

The beast leaned back on its haunches and roared up at the sun. Birds took to the sky from the surrounding treetops, and little Johnny's broken body slumped to the timothy.

Madison watched with a hand across her mouth. Her family was dead, of that she was certain, and the thing down there—a thing which should not be—was their murderer.

Her instincts told her to run, to put as much distance between herself and the monster as possible, but she was too frightened, too angry, too distraught to even begin to think about moving.

It wasn't until the beast began to scale the hill, loping toward her with a twisted, almost alien gait, that she knew she had to run, had to get away from it, had to make it back to the Plymouth. The people of Cobalt needed to hear about this thing, and hear about it from a reliable source, not the drunken lips of the local lunatic.

She turned and ran, screaming all the way across the crest of the hill. Past the picnic hamper she went, and the tree underneath which she had been languidly daydreaming only a few minutes ago.

Behind her the creature roared.

And Johnny was dead.

Ethan, too.

The creature roared again.

And Ethan had brought them up here for a family picnic, and now this!

It roared again.

The car, Madison thought, was too far away; there was no way she was going to make it. And that was when she turned her ankle on a rock jutting out of the hill.

Told you so!

Madison went down as a sharp pain made its way from her toes all the way up to her back. White dots danced between her eyes and eyelids as she cursed everything about Cobalt, and cursed

1,212 residents for not taking Burt McCarthy seriously.

And now her family was dead.

The creature, so close now that she felt the ground shake beneath her fallen body with each step it took, was not sated, would not be sated until it had her beneath its colossal feet, her skull ground to a fine powder.

She screamed a final time, and then her vision was filled with yellow. Golden-yellow hair, and at its centre nothing but darkness and teeth. It was the closest thing to a demon Madison had ever seen.

She hoped and prayed, as it picked her up from the grass and began to squeeze her until her skeleton overlapped inside of her, for a quick and painless death.

She was afforded neither.

IV

Article from Toronto Star, April 15th, 2017

> The bodies of several missing hikers were discovered yesterday near Cobalt, Ontario. Villagers discovered the remains near Sasaginaga Lake at around 12:30pm. The bodies are believed to be that of Michael and Cherry Gagnon, as well as David Tremblay and Victoria Cote. They were found not far from where they were reported to have vanished last month, despite the police

carrying out a thorough search of the area at the time of the disappearance.

Commissioner Fred Anderson of the Ontario Provincial Police has urged calm, following these latest murders.

"Remain vigilant, and steer clear of Cobalt Lode and the surrounding area unless absolutely necessary."

When questioned about a possible link between these new remains and Old Yellow Top, the legendary creature said to stalk the area, the commissioner refused to comment.

These four bodies take the total number of deaths in Cobalt and the district of Timiskaming to ninety-eight since records began.

A Day In The Life of A Cactus Cat

Lauren E Reynolds

He woke up in a cage.

He knew what it was for all beasts knew what the dreaded human trap was called. He felt the cold steel press against his cheek and identified the vague outline of iron bars. Groggy, he shook his head, clearing his vision and swiped the landscape with a quick glance. Shapes and shadows returned to recognizable things: cactus, mountains, canyons.

Then he saw them: with their ugly faces scrunched deep against the bars and their beady eyes gleaming with horrified wonderment.

He sprang to his feet, hissing a ferocious cry like the howl of a murderous hunter. He struck his tail across the bars like a club but the ugly creatures retreated too quickly and he missed the sensitive facial flesh.

Where was he? How had he gotten there? And how far away was he? He did not know and his mind scrambled for answers. He had to get back, he realized. Before it happened, if it hadn't already? Now the question was how?

"Well," one of the creatures chuckled half-awed and half-appalled. "Ain't that just the beatinest thing I ever did see?"

The other's face scrunched up in disgusted curiosity. "I reckon it is, but what the Sam Hill kind of critter is it?"

"What are ya blind? What kind of critter is it? It's a bobcat, ya ninny! Can't you hear it? Hissing like the devil himself?"

"Bobcat nothing! That critter's a porcupine!"

"A porcupine? Did you hit your head?"

"I'm serious! Look at it, will ya! What kind of cat has spikes on its tail and quills in its fur! I'm tellin ya, it's a porcupine!"

"Porcupine my Aunt Sally! Porcupines ain't got teeth and claws like that! And see those tuffs of hair coming out of its legs? It's a bobcat, no mistake!"

"Those ain't tuffs, they're bones! Or spikes! Or something, but that critter ain't no cat!"

He watched them bicker and point out his appendages. Scrutinizing for escapes, he sniffed the air. The sun was high, making it difficult for his nocturnal eyes, but he smelled the hot sand and the sweet tang of cacti nearby and relief flooded through him. So they hadn't taken him from the desert. Now the question was how long had he been asleep? And how far had they gone? And there was still the lingering question of how he had ended up there. His mind searched for answers but no memories came. He licked his canines, tasting the sweet fermented juice of saguaro cactus. His eyes flew open.

That's right. He remembered now. He had been hunting, a routine trip: scouting their territory, renewing the scent markings, and slashing the cacti. On the hunt back he'd found one already open and its slimy juice thickened to sap that clung to its needles. He'd lapped at them greedily, relishing the sweetness. His hunt forgotten, he had drunk until he was intoxicated. Then he had rolled giddily in the sand and shrieked into the night, pouncing and prancing until he'd pranced right into a trap and passed out from shock and exhaustion.

He hissed, furious with himself. How worried she must've been when the sun arose and he'd yet to come home. Was he too late? Quickly, searching for an escape, he jumped when the two creatures yelled, exchanging angry noises and throwing their broad, flat paws up in rage.

"I don't care what it is! Point is we can't skin it! And if we can't skin it, we can't sell it! No Lady in her right mind is gonna wanna wear a coat of cactus quills!"

"Na, we can't skin it, but maybe we can sell it. Or show it! Yeah, that's it! Think of how many people'll line up to get a glimpse of the legendary porcupine cat?"

His ears went straight, all his spines erect. So that was it: they weren't just trappers, they were skinners: the worst of the creatures and their lot. And now they hoped to make him some sideshow for others of their kind? No, this would not be his fate! He would make it home. He had too.

A plan formed; he collapsed on his side and moaned pitifully.

"Now what's it doing?"

He moaned louder, favoring a limp paw curled at its side.

"It is hurt?

"One way to find out." One of them leaned down towards the cage and fiddled with the lock.

"You ain't lettin that thing out? It'll cause a havoc!"

"Quit your bellyaching you ninny, can't you see its hurt?"

He held perfectly still as the creature hesitantly moved a hand towards it. He licked its finger. It wrapped its flat, hairless paw against its cheek. He nuzzled it, purring contently. It wrapped its cold, fleshly paws around his waist and lifted him from the cage. He stayed still.

"There ya see?" the creature bragged.

He came to life at that moment. He bit down hard on the brute's hand and slapped it across the forearm with its tail, leaving angry, red, branch-shaped welts. The creature howled with pain and nursed his wounded arm, dropping him. With a single arch, he spun and elegantly landed on all four feet.

The other creature panicked and grabbed frightfully for a shotgun, another creature creation all beasts knew, but he was faster. He pounced towards it biting, clawing and striking at his feet. The creature danced out of the way, narrowly avoiding his claws. It tripped, stumbled and screamed, firing a shot harmlessly into the air.

He sprang over the spineless lump and dashed into the cacti forests with an ear-splitting howl of remembrance into the rising day. He did not look back and they did not follow him.

Once he was a safe distance away, he stopped and surveyed the canyon, but it was different in the sunlight. What was familiar in the shadows at night was frighteningly alien and almost eerie by day. He sniffed the air, the dirt, the nearby cactus for familiar traces, then stopped. His nostrils filled with the rich pungent smell of something recognizable but the scent was not hit own.

A fierce roar and sharp points in his back confirmed his fears. Pounced upon and caught off guard he was forced to the ground and rolled to get his attacker off him. The sharp claws shook free and he rolled into a standing position, narrowly avoiding the slashing claws and spiked tail of his adversary whose territory he'd wondered into. Coming face to face with another of his kind, he hissed, claws flexed and spines erect. Appearing bigger and more frightening, they circled each other, tails flickering, threatening, their barbs and prongs evenly matched. Then his opponent pounced, tail striking like a scorpion. He rolled out of the way then leaped, sinking his teeth deep into the other's neck. His competitor yowled, momentarily stunned and they rolled across the ground. Quickly, he leaped away, leaving his adversary on the ground. Sacrificing victory, he sprinted headlong into the desert. This was no time for territorial disputes.

He had to find Home.

He traveled all day and well into the evening, following a faint scent he knew well. At last he stumbled upon a familiar setting and gazed delightedly at the towering saguaro: their bases scarred with slashes and bleeding thick sap. Dehydrated from his long journey, he sniffed the pungent sweetness and lapped greedily at the thick juice. The tangy taste filled his mouth and nose, commanding him to drink more, but his memory was persistent and urged him on. He slashed his tail across a fresh cactus and drank the flowing, watery juice. It was a cool but bitter sweetness against his tongue though not as sweet as the fermented sap, but it quenched his thirst and refreshed his senses.

Dusk fell heavy over the desert and the denizens of darkness abandoned their shelters to hunt in the cool night. He was no exception. He couldn't go home without a kill after all.

He waited patiently, ears twitching at the slightest sound. His nocturnal eyes saw everything bright as daylight. A scurry and a hiss and he found his quarry: a large scorpion poised to kill a mouse. Crawling on his belly, his approach was silent. The mouse spied him first and fled, just as he pounced on the bemused scorpion.

It did not surrender quietly, for scorpions are audacious arachnids. Even trapped between his paws, it waved his menacing claws and arrogantly struck his paw with its poison tail.

It did nothing.

Showing it a real spike, he struck the scorpion with his own tail, piercing armor and exoskeleton. Stunned, the scorpion didn't register the hole in its back and stumbled about dazed, then died.

He grinned proudly and carried it home. But first he needed something else. Before departing, he returned to the cactus and punctured the thick skin with his tail: piercing and slashed until a large chunk hung from the barbs of his tail. There is hung, safely away from his nose and mouth. Its intoxicating trick useless. He wouldn't let it trick him twice.

At last, he journeyed home.

Past and through the cacti forest marked by his claws and scent. Past the deep fissure in the canyon and the dried up tumbleweeds where he hunted scorpions and mice. And past the towering triangular rocks that looked like those flimsy shelters the creatures built for themselves. At last, he came upon the ruins of a once proud and ancient saguaro that had long sense fallen, broken and been hollowed out.

He approached cautiously, suddenly skittish like a kitten too afraid to face his curiosity. He stopped at the entrance, dropped the scorpion and asked permission with a soft meow.

She heard him at once and spun to him. Her beautiful spines bristled with delight and the worry in her bright eyes was replaced with joy. He bounded over to her, ecstatically and nuzzled her face with his own. She returned the gesture with just as much affection memorizing his face with her whiskers. He nudged his kill towards her and she thanked him with a soft purr.

They would share it later, she promised.

She rolled slightly, presenting her belly which was flocked by three squirming bodies. His eyes bulged with delight and he licked her cheek, proudly. Stepping inside, he pressed his nose to their soft sides. They squeaked and mewed, timidly at first, but then calmed at the sound of his soft purring. They greeted him with tiny wet noses and tiny licks and meowed delightedly, but hungrily. He swished his tail and presented his bounty. They followed their noses and smelled the juice, licking and climbing over each other for a taste.

Settling down next to his mate, he watched his kittens as they played and feasted. His eyes alighted with pride. Though their eyes were closed and their fur had not yet grown spikes, already they knew *he* was their father, already they recognized the cactus juice.

One day, they would grow spikes and fangs. One day, their tails would grow branch-like and barbed. One day, they would hunt scorpions, and slash saguaro, and defend their territories from others of their kind, and outwit those witless creatures who invaded the desert with cages and traps. One day, under their mother's watchful eye and his strict tutelage, they would become fierce and ferocious Cactus Cats.

Two Yurts
Dale L. Sproule

Through the crack in the curtain at the foot of his bed, Troy saw shadows, shifting. A loud noise had awakened him and he searched through the shallow haze of his memory for a clue to its nature: a roar, a shout, a scream?

Now, furrowing his brow at new sounds – the plopping and slithering of something ponderous, dragging itself across the floor, Troy heard himself shout, "Run," but when he threw back the sheets, he couldn't run, or even move. Tubes were tunneling through layers of bandages and into his belly, in a dozen places. A weight tugged on his cock from the inside. He gagged and pulled at the tube that entered his nose and ran down his throat, like a fish that had swallowed a hook.

His gut felt cold and hollow. There were beeps and flashing lights from the machines that hunched over the bed.

"You okay?" A groggy male voice seeped through the curtain that ran down the side of the bed. It was his neighbor in this place – clearly a hospital ward. The noise that had awakened

Troy, must have startled this guy awake as well.

"Did you hear that too?" Troy wanted to ask, but nothing came out of him but the fluids gurgling through the tubes. He tried again, "Thawslauwastha?"

But somehow, the guy seemed to understand. "I hear it too. All night long. Nurse says it's the respirator in the bed by the window…." As the guy kept talking, his voice became a comforting drone. The pain ebbed away and sleep pulled Troy back under. "…but that bed is empty," were the last words he heard before the curtains opened with a rasp and a rattle and diffuse morning light poured in.

"Oh, good, you're awake," came a woman's voice, as a Filipino woman in her fifties entered and brusquely started straightening his sheets.

Trying to respond, he found himself again pulling at the tubes. The nurse held his arms down to his sides, as though restraining a toddler. "Don't do that. You'll hurt yourself."

As the hospital milieu reestablished itself, Troy tried to ask, "How did I get here?" But even he couldn't understand the sounds that actually came out. He slowed down, and managed to croak a single intelligible syllable, "Drink?"

"Not 'til your doctor comes in." After checking the bags

on the IV, she clamped something to his fingertip. "But maybe I can get you some ice to suck on."

As the tiny shard melted on his tongue, he gave up all ambition to speak, and before he knew it, was awakening from sleep again with someone pulling back the bandages. This must be the doctor. Troy struggled to stay awake, and saw his chest and belly punctured, slashed and torn, in a strange pattern, as if someone had tried to carve some sort of symmetrical rune into his abdomen. It was red and blue and yellow with blood and bruises and the tinctures slathered on during surgery. It looked raw and horrible and Troy was totally at a loss to remember how this had happened or what had done it to him. By the time he was alert enough to ask questions, the wound was bandaged back up again and the doctor was gone. He tried to call her back but his voice sounded like formless mewling. So he slept instead.

A different nurse explained that he couldn't eat until they were sure about the extent of his injuries. As she adjusted his morphine drip, she said, "Soon, we'll give you a button, so you can give yourself the pain killers."

The food smells that woke him next, said it was lunchtime, but it turned out to be dinner.

Instead of feeding him, they introduced him to a woman

in a suit. "Detective LaGrande," she said. "No one can tell me what sort of weapon was used in your attack. What do you remember?"

Now that was a question. His name was Troy. His wife Kim had recently left him, or more precisely kicked his unemployed ass out of the apartment. And he took the first job that came along in the hopes of winning her back. He and Kim had a baby daughter, Zuzee, who was with her mom. And Kim's new boyfriend. Fuck, fuck, fuck. He lived with them now. *Despite* Troy's new job with CloudNine Property Management.

His horticulture degree was useless. They'd hired him for his size. He thought he'd come so far, and he was back to being a bouncer. "The Evictor" – one of his new co-workers had laughingly called him before one of the senior managers, Michael Verser, took him to see some tenants at Easter Avenue Mall. Along with a head cold, and some grave reservations, Troy had three tenants to evict along the concourse.

He remembered walking into the first of the shops, its name stenciled on the door in three languages. The only one Troy recognized was English – *Culturu Horhai* – an English alphabet if not English words. Verser called it "the Mongolian shop."

The air was thick with incense and the narrow aisles were

full of exotic trinkets: metal sequins, silver belts, knives, swords, spearheads, gongs, shields and strange hijabs and helmets, colorful fabrics in geometric patterns and brassware depicting horses and dragons and suns and camels and birds of prey.

Each section of the store was separated by different colored curtains. Wondering if it contravened fire regulations, Troy pushed onward into the heart of the store until he reached the clerk at the counter – a youngish Asian man with a pleasant smile.

Troy remembered asking, "Are you the owner?" And then opening his eyes to find himself here.

His ability to form and use words had improved throughout the day. So he shared what he could remember with the detective. When Troy suggested, "Talk to my boss, Michael Verser," she just looked at him with sad eyes and shook her head. Then she was gone and there was a new nurse, some doctors and orderlies, another food cart, more nurses. And when he awoke, feeling awake and semi-lucid for the first time in ages, the light was fading. His curtain was open at the end and there were visitors crowded round the bed on the opposite side of the room. This puzzled him because he'd been told that all the other patients had been moved.

Troy peered into the tent-like enclosure against the far wall. It made him think of a kind of tent he'd seen in a movie one time – a yurt. There were two chairs at the foot of his bed and two at the side, plus a number of people standing…too many visitors to count. Why would the hospital allow this many?

The man in the bed seemed familiar, although much older than the person Troy was struggling to recall.

His guests didn't leave when an unfamiliar nurse came to change his dressings and empty the collected discharge from the plastic sacs through which his bodily fluids were being diverted.

"Good evening, Mr. Khorkoi," the nurse voiced the pleasantries to the patient in a dutiful tone.

The visitors actually drew in closer as the procedure began. In a macabre call and response, the patient's tortured moans as each wound was uncovered and irrigated, were answered by collective gasps and sighs from the onlookers.

When the nurse left, their voices resumed murmuring, in a language Troy didn't understand. He closed his eyes, and when he opened them again, his own curtain was closed and the room was dark. The voices, no longer a constant babble, were now whispering like prairie grasses in a gusting wind. Rising and falling, less like conversation than chanting.

When he summoned a nurse and asked about the man and all his visitors and she shrugged and informed him in a Caribbean accent. "Dat bed is empty. Mistah Cruther move out dis morning. Deys nobody dere all day."

"Not Mr. Caruthers, Mr. Khorkoi. That's what the other nurse called him – the older one. There were lots of people, making noise…chanting."

"Dere's all kindsa sound in de hospi-tal." She said with a smiling finality.

He eventually fell back to sleep, but hadn't slept long when he was again awakened by the chanting, which had grown considerably louder. He managed to hook the bed table with his fingertips and swing it over. He fished his cell phone out of the drawer and checked the time. 3:23 am. Far too late for this nonsense.

In the eons it took for the night nurse to answer the page, Troy fell asleep again. She was checking his pulse as he awakened. After a cursory check of the IV, she went to leave.

"Would you mind leaving my curtain open?" He asked, and she pulled it open wider.

The curtain of the empty bed across the way was closed – an odd thing to do with an empty bed.

As he lay there staring at it in the wan light from the window and the hall, the curtain seemed to move, as if pushed out from within, as though the crowd had returned.

Troy raised his bed to a sitting position and swung his legs over the edge. He had been to the bathroom that afternoon, but it was much worse with no one to help him. Pain filled his entire abdomen. He couldn't draw in a whole breath, or even half of one. As he fought down a wave of dizziness and disorientation, he realized he didn't have the strength to either stand or pull his legs back up onto the bed. The page button was pinned to the raised portion of his bed, at the very top. He reached for it, twisting and stretching until it felt like his torso was tearing in half, but fell short. He was sweating and shaking and embarrassed about the position he had gotten himself into, unable to move forward or back. Even lying down was too painful. Ashamed at the sound he finally recognized as his own whimpering, he leaned over and closed his eyes. He gathered enough composure to try again and got one leg back up before running out of steam.

He looked up again and saw that a light had come on behind the curtain across the way. Not the usual light though. This was more like a candle, flickering. Or possibly several candles. The curtain began to open. *It's empty,* he told himself. *You're imagining this.*

That bed too was upright, mirroring Troy's own. But that bed was surrounded by supplicants on their knees. The bed, somehow, looked more like a throne. The patient was wrapped in bandages. Not much detail was visible, but he didn't seem to have any arms. He leaned forward and Troy saw the only unbandaged spot, at the top of his head, growing larger. As if his hair was growing. No. It wasn't hair. It was an orifice – a giant mouth, opening. Filled with pointed teeth. The thing wasn't a bandaged man, it was an immense larva – an eyeless, faceless worm that opened its mandala mouth wide, creating a shape that was a perfect match for the wounds on Troy's chest and belly. Unable to flee or even raise an alarm, Troy opened his mouth to scream, but all that came out was a croak. He closed his eyes, trying to convince himself that this was just some sort of drug-induced nightmare. But he knew it wasn't something his had just conjured up, it was something he'd seen. Not a dream, it was a memory of what he'd seen inside that store. He kept his eyes clamped shut, listening to the sounds slithering toward him.As he reached an absolute state of voiceless terror, with nowhere to run, unconsciousness became the only place he could flee. But even sleep was full of nightmares.

He was actually surprised to wake up in the morning. He felt lost and ashamed, although he wasn't sure what he was ashamed of.

There was a gentle knock on the door and when he looked up, he felt a sudden shock of dislocation and a rising sense of dread. It was Mr. Khorkoi from the bed across the way, only now, he was looking totally healthy and mobile – as though twenty years younger than he had looked when Troy had seen him surrounded by supplicants.

Again, Troy was overcome with a sense of helpless panic. The nurses were getting used to his hysterics. They might not even come if he pushed the help button. And even if they came, it would take them far, far too long to save him from what was about to happen. The man entered the room, took several steps toward the bed. Troy swallowed back a scream.

"I hope you're feeling better," Khorkoi said, pleasantly.

"What? Why would you care?"

The man smiled. "I'm sorry, I should have introduced myself. I am Tse Nergui Zaya. You've been in my store, Culturu Horhai. I'm sorry I wasn't there when you came in. And about what happened to Mr. Verser."

Troy had far too many questions. The first one that made it out of his mouth was, "What happened to Mr. Verser? The police wouldn't say…"

The man shook his head. "He died from his burns."

"Burns? If there was a fire, why am I not burned? What happened to me? Why wouldn't they tell me anything?"

"Because they don't know anything. They think your colleague was burned by some sort of acid. They don't know about the worm's toxin."

"Worm? What are you talking about?"

"The Olgoi-Khorkai is one of the black tngri – an ancient god, we thought long dead. A spirit that made sense in our nomadic culture, before the great Khans, but has no place in the modern world."

Troy found himself objecting to this statement, deep inside, although he couldn't say why. The man's words actually made him angry.

Zaya went on. "The Olgoi-Khorkai spits a deadly toxin that supposedly melts a man's flesh right off his bones. We think that's what happened to your friend."

"He wasn't my friend." Troy said, biting back the words, *I have no friends anymore.* "And what you're saying makes no sense.

Why would it kill him and not me? What happened to me?"

The Asian man shook his head, looking less and less familiar as the conversation progressed.

"Little is known. No one imagined that this creature survived. Until we were confronted by the evidence. But we think it chose you."

"Chose me for what?"

Zaya shrugged. "Someone, in my community – a scholar – a shaman of sorts, suggested that perhaps it recognized a kindred spirit in you. Someone as spiritually homeless as it is."

"I'm not homeless!" Troy bridled.

"*Spiritually…*" But even as this man, this Dennis, tried to set him straight, Troy admitted deep down inside that it was at least partially true. He had given up the friends and family he'd grown up with, to come to Toronto with Kim, and he'd stayed here because he wanted his baby daughter to know her real Dad. But now, besides caring for his child every second weekend, he had nothing to live for anymore; no home, no real family, not even a proper job in his field, since his Horticulture background and five years of experience with Parks and Rec in Windsor didn't translate to anything here.

Everyone he had cared about had faded away, become

less and less a part of his life. He felt much more like an evictee than an evictor.

"You need to reject this creature! To push it out!" Zaya was saying.

And somehow the notion that he could save some near-extinct creature by allowing it to take up residence inside of him – appealed to the naturalist part of his nature, the part of Troy that had led him to take up horticulture in the first place.

Maybe there was a place for him after all – someone, or at least something that *needed* him, that valued him. He thought about all the other disenfranchised people in the world and realized that maybe the Olgoi-Korkai's real time was now. That the ancient stuff was merely a prelude.

He looked back up at his visitor, who was red faced as he explained how the abomination that was the Death Worm couldn't be allowed to live. And Troy felt repulsed. The acid reflux he'd been experiencing for the past few days was acting up again. Bile filled his gorge, burned its way up his throat and bubbled up into his mouth.

He tried to swallow it back, which made him choke. A gobbet of phlegm dripped down his chin, pooling on his sheet. He watched, fascinated, as it smoldered and burnt through the sturdy fabric like the ember from a cigarette.

And when he looked back up, he saw his guest turning the corner and fleeing down the hall. "Who needs him," Troy thought. "Who needs any of them?"

When he had gazed upon the creature during the night, and had felt so repulsed and petrified by fear, he simply hadn't understood. There was nothing to fear – ever again. The time had come round again, the time for *being* feared – for reawakening the awe and worship the Olgoi-Korkai had once inspired.

He threw back he sheets and looked down at his bandages. Not only would he soon be healed – he would be whole again, for the first time in a very, very long time. And there was no reason, no reason at all, that he couldn't live forever.

An Exchange of Fear

Lynn Rushlau

Wrapping a scarf around her face, Taigan braced herself and pushed the door open. Thick, fat snowflakes poured from the sky. Snow drifts completely obscured the steps, but the porch could be swept clean.

She squinted towards the Silver Ibis Gate while she worked, and was pretty sure she caught a speck of green in the air, the "all's well" flag. Thank the Goddess. She'd hate to have to ski up to the Temple in this.

Porch swept clean, she made a face at the steps. Her job required her to keep them clear, but really who was going to ski over for a visit today? Even the porch had been overkill. Already the wind blew snow back into place.

Not that it mattered. No one would be visiting. A whistling swoosh cut through the soft patter of falling snow.

Heart rocketing, she scrambled to the door. Afraid to turn her back, she squinted into the storm while her hand flailed for the knob behind her. Too much snow fell too thickly. She couldn't see anything. It could be one big step out of sight.

She caught the handle & yanked hard enough to fling the door open and herself off balance. She tumbled to the lobby floor. Shooting to her feet, she slammed the door. It lacked a lock. Shouldn't matter. Ignoring the pangs shooting from her elbow and hip, she stomped snow off her boots and struggled to remove her outer garments with shaking hands. Her heart continued to beat in triple-time, even as she left the lobby and locked the interior door behind her.

She walked through the blissfully warm room to her bedroom. Both cats remained curled up on the bed. She petted them, taking deep breaths to still her panic. It couldn't get in. She was safe and secure in the Receiving House of the Temple Abyes.

With the weather, she'd run out of administrative work. Couldn't expect to review any visitors needing access to the Temple or its staff in hopes of help with one of the Goddess' creatures. She'd mopped yesterday. Swept the kitchen after her dinner. All she really need do today was start a loaf of bread for tonight's meal and that could wait until afternoon.

Simply to prove she'd done something with her day, she

ran a dust rag over her bedroom furniture and then the office. The chore used up less than an hour of her day as everything had been spotless already.

Grinning, she returned to the office, claimed her favorite seat in front of the fire and picked up a novel. Another whistle swooshed through the air. She dropped her book. Stared wide-eyed at her shuttered window. It was outside. It couldn't get in. Had no reason to want to. She had no reason to go out to it. Shuddering, she exhaled slowly and retrieved the book and bookmark.

The abominable whistled again as she sat up. Her heart thumped loudly in her ears. She tried for her next breath, but her chest constricted. Perhaps two creatures passed nearby and were simply communicating? Black spots danced before her eyes. She forced herself to take one breath. Another. Slow and steady.

When no further swooshes filled the air, she flipped back through the book to find her place. Hand splayed across the page, she cocked her head to the side and listened.

The stout walls of the Receiving House muffled the soft patter of falling snow. She'd have to go back to the lobby and open the door to confirm it still fell since the windows were shuttered inside and out this deep into winter. The fire crackling in the hearth prevented utter silence from filling the room. Smiling, she turned her attention to her book.

A thump from without startled her. Her fingers tightened on the book. One couldn't get in. The abominables were simply too big to fit through the door. A series of thumps followed by a clatter. Someone laughed.

She exhaled in a laugh at herself. Someone had skied down from Temple Abyes. Likely Eolan brought her more reports to log.

Rising, she crossed to the lobby. Her greeting died on her lips. Three kids stomped on mats, divesting themselves of scarves and hats.

Several bursts of outrage tumbled through her mind. "Please tell me you did not sneak out."

"We left with permission. I swear." Briah, a teaching assistant in her early twenties, grinned at Taigan as she swatted snow off her shoulders. "Valene, keep the coat on. It'll be freezing upstairs."

Taigan glanced at the adolescent girl who shrugged her coat back on before turning to Briah. Taigan shook her head at the younger woman. "Upstairs?"

"The guards picked up abominable calls. Surely you

heard them?" Briah asked. Valene and the boy who'd disrobed enough to be identified as Keil looked sharply her direction.

"Of course. Which makes skiing down here in white-out conditions all the more dangerous."

"We used the crystal body-heat scanners before we set out. They're a few miles out, but looked to be heading this way, so Sarlana gave us permission to ski down and watch them pass."

They could have done the same from a guard tower without risking frostbite and getting lost in the blizzard. Though at this time of year, the towers were shuttered and the guards would be watching through mirrors. All windows would be closed up as tight as hers.

Taigan huffed at the sheer idiocy of those with snow creature affinities. "You'll freeze to death up there."

The three grinned at her.

"We brought charcoal warmers and were hoping to borrow blankets." Briah nodded to the door in northeast corner. Keil crossed to it with Valene on his heels.

"Of course. I'll bring some up." Back in the office, she swung the kettle over the fire before going to the linen closet and pulling out a stack of thick blankets.

Briah and the kids already had the shutters pulled back

from two windows when she got upstairs. Shivering, she dumped the blankets beside their pile of bags. "I've set water to boil. Any preference on tea?"

"Ooh, thank you. Peppermint, please." Briah looked over her shoulder from the shutter she was busy opening. "These two don't need any caffeine."

Valene and Keil exchanged disagreeing scowls.

Arms wrapped tightly around herself, Taigan crossed to the nearest window and peered out. Couldn't imagine how they hoped to watch anything in this. She squinted. Couldn't see a damned thing but snowflakes and too many of those to actually pick out individual ones. She shivered again.

"Let me know if you need anything. I'll bring the tea up once it's ready."

Bracing herself, Taigan pulled on a second sweater, a hat, and her fingerless gloves to carry the tray upstairs. For the last half hour, loud whistling swooshes had filled the air. Another one nearly made her to drop the tray two steps from the top. Heart racketing about in her chest, she entered the attic and set the tray on the work table against the wall near the door. The three huddled around the front window, wrapped up in their blankets.

"Is it visible?" she asked.

"Oh, yes," Valene breathed. She scribbled quickly in a notebook. Keil and Briah did the same. Taigan stepped up behind Briah and looked at what she'd written. *Hurt. Hurt. Help. Intruders. Kill. Kill. Help.*

"That's terrible." Taigan squinted out the window. She could make out a dark shape at the limits of her sight. She shuddered. "Just the one?"

"So far."

"What could have hurt it?"

"Tons of things," Keil answered. "Dragons, griffins, anything bigger than it really."

"Or humans," Valene said.

"There shouldn't be anyone in the abominables' territory," Keil said.

"Doesn't mean there aren't," Valene pointed out.

"Can you help it?" Taigan asked. She might be terrified of them, but she wouldn't wish pain on any of the Goddess' creatures.

All three looked at her as if she were a bit mad. Or more than a bit the look on Briah's face suggested. Valene cursed under her breath. Taigan glanced at her to ask, but followed her gaze outside. The dark blob had disappeared from sight.

"We can't go chasing it. And the three of us are hardly a qualified medical team," Briah said.

Taigan nodded. She understood that. Teams in the field rendered assistance when possible. But those would be adults with experience, not kids still learning. In a blizzard. There'd be teams up at the Temple, but getting the message to them that assistance was needed would be complicated. Still.

"Should I run up a flag?"

Briah hesitated before waving at the window. "If it comes back this way perhaps, but we have no reason to assume it will."

Taigan watched with them for a few minutes, but the dark blob was in no hurry to reappear and the attic was freezing. She left them to it. Briah said they'd come down for lunch so Taigan headed off get a meal started.

After a riotous meal filled with the latest Temple gossip, the youngsters offered to wash up. They'd crossed to the sink with their first armload of dishes when an ear-piercing whistle cut through their chatter. The building shook. Great snaps of splintering wood were followed by two whistling swooshes.

The cats fled. Valene and Keil dropped the dishes next to the sink and turned to Briah. Eyes wide, she faced Taigan. "Where are the spears?"

Taigan stared back at her through another crash. They weren't supposed to injure creatures. Ever. "Can't you talk to it?"

"There's two and they're battle-mad."

"Are we going to kill them?" Valene asked in a small voice.

"Of course not," Briah snapped. "Taigan, get the spears. We may need them to keep the abominables back enough to talk to us."

"Wouldn't fire be better?" Keil asked.

"You're not burning down my Receiving House," Taigan said.

"Upstairs, everyone. It'll be safest," Briah ordered. Grabbing her coat, she pivoted and darted through the door. Valene hurried after her.

"I'll help with the spears." Keil followed Taigan into the hall towards her bedroom. She flung open the supply closet.

"There are only three." She handed all of them to Keil and turned to a chest on the left as he raced out of the room. She flipped back the lid of a wooden box on the center shelf and considered the flares. How many might they need? Technically one would alert the Temple to their need, but with weather conditions--another great snap of wood. This one was followed by shattering glass. No time to think, she snapped the lid shut and shoved the entire box under her arm.

The white wooly fur of an abominable's leg poked through the wall. A glance down revealed a clawed blue foot half as wide as she was tall standing in the shattered remnants of the Receiving House's porch. She backed into the wall. Wanted to faint. Wanted to vomit. To do both at the same time.

The box of flares spilled from her numb hands. She couldn't do this. Could not. This was insane. Too insane. She should be hiding under the bed with the cats. They were the smart ones here.

A truncated scream overhead cut through her shock. She had to get help. Had to send the signal. The flares had scattered everywhere and retrieving them involved moving closer to the abominable. Another scream. Shouting. Words she couldn't understand.

They needed her.

Sweating terribly despite the cold, she darted forward and seized the nearest flare. Vomit rose in her throat when she bent over. Swallowing it back, she stumbled towards the stairs. Grabbed another next to the door. Praying the house was not about to come down on them, she scrambled up the rocking staircase.

The bones fell out of her legs at the head of the stairs. She gripped the doorjamb as black dots swirled in front of her eyes.

It would eat them all.

Briah whistled at it. Taigan blinked and could see more than the abominable's teeth. Keil and Valene aimed spears at its face. Hers resting in the crook of her arm, Briah stood between the spear tips. The jagged fangs the creature gnashed at them were as long as her forearm. It whistled back, filling the room with the unbearable stench of a slaughterhouse. Briah whistled again. Roaring, the abominable tore off another piece of the wall.

Though not a sound escaped her lips, Taigan screamed for help. It was trying to climb inside, but wasn't quite tall enough. And was too strong. Its attempts merely ripped up the house instead of pulling it inside. She squeaked, startled herself, and nearly dropped the flares.

Oh.

She was the one who had to call for help. Whimpering under her breath, she pressed against the wall, scooted around to the window behind the cluster of humans, and flung the shutters open. They banged and bounced off the wall.

"What are you doing?" Valene turned.

"Alerting the Temple." Sweat trickled down her back and froze along its path.

"Shut up, both of you," Briah hissed before whistling again.

Though it took four attempts, Taigan cranked open the window. The change to the temperature shouldn't have been dramatic. The hole the abominable created already exposed the room to the elements. But the new opening gave the wind a course to flow through. With unsteady fingers, she bashed the end of a flare on the window sill. It shot into the sky. The Temple guards shouldn't miss that bright orange light.

Though she needed to watch for a response from the Temple, Taigan couldn't help but turn back to the abominable. Couldn't stand to have it behind her and not know what it was doing. See where it might move. Know if it reached out to grab her.

Briah whistled and the abominable let go of the house, taking a step back. Briah whistled again. The abominable's reply was low and mournful.

"You're mad," Valene hissed as Briah backed towards the door. The abominable disappeared from view with a crunch of wood. Keil followed Briah down the stairs.

"What's going on?" Taigan asked.

"She's going outside to help them."

"WHAT?"

But Valene grabbed a backpack and disappeared through the doorway. Cursing, Taigan turned back to the window. A responding flare hovered over the gate. Praise the Goddess, they'd seen her distress flare. Help was on the way.

Second flare in her pocket, she followed, unsure where she was headed. Safety and hiding? Or outside to witness the madness? She would be no help. No reason for her to follow them outside. She was an admin, not a creature specialist. She had no medical training for humans, let alone creatures. Her job was to interview people. Delegate them to the right people at the Temple who could help them. That person was never going to be her.

She reached the lobby and stood in the ruins, still clueless over her next course of action. The whistles from outside were low. More like conversation now instead of an exchange of fear and threats. She could see nothing from here. That was good, she told herself. She didn't want to see the creatures.

Except not knowing what was going on out there left her more fearful than peeking through a hole would. She eased her way over the debris that used to be her lobby.

A second abominable lay prone in the snow. Brilliant red blood smeared across its leg and chest. Three broken bits of wood protruded from the seeping wounds. Arrows. Taigan winced. Humans.

The two abominables whistled softly at each other. Briah stood, hip deep in the snow, mere steps away from the shattered porch with Keil and Valene right behind her. Bag dangling from her hand, Valene gestured for Taigan to join them.

Why? Her lips moved, but she couldn't voice the question.

Still, they weren't supposed to be dealing with something like this. They were too young. As the oldest person present, she felt obligated to attempt to protect them. Though she knew the idea that she would be any help was ridiculous, she stepped through the wall and crossed the porch.

Valene trudged over and held out a hand to help her down. The abominable on the ground swooshed with gusto, but the whistle ended in a mournful tone. Briah whistled an answer. Taigan glanced at Valene, who grimaced.

"She's telling them that it'll hurt but she must remove the arrows. It's a hard concept to translate. They sense familiar

Temple smells on us so they want to trust us, but don't since humans shot them."

Briah stepped closer to the fallen creature. Taigan's head spun. The abominable whistled pitifully to the upright one, which now squatted down, whistling a long stream of soft swooshes. Briah knelt beside the arrow in its leg and whistled at the uninjured abominable. It came around and held its friend's legs. Briah removed a knife from her bag.

Whistling shrilly, both abominables started to rise. Briah and Keil whistled back. Taigan clutched Valene's arm hard enough to bruise. The girl pried her fingers free. "They're telling them it's okay. The knife is needed to cut the arrows free," she whispered quickly.

Briah cut into the leg beside the broken arrow shaft. The abominable's leg shot out, caught Briah in the chest, and sent her flying a good ten feet away. Both creatures roared at the humans. Holding his hands up, Keil whistled back. With a gasp, Valene shot to his side.

Taigan barely noticed. Briah, an unmoving heap in the snow, was all she could see. She forgot about the monsters. Forgot everything, but Briah. Taigan fought her way through snow to her. Heard her groans with relief. Briah was attempting to sit up. Taigan held her in place.

"Maybe you shouldn't move."

"The abominable needs help."

"The kids are talking to it." The whistles behind her definitely came from humans as well as abominables.

"They need help. Get me up. Help me back over there," Briah ordered.

Taigan glanced over in time to watch Valene toss a bloody arrow to the ground.

"They have it under control, and there's help on the way." Taigan nodded towards the Temple where a dozen skiers poured through the gates. Nothing was going force her to move closer to those creatures.

Briah cursed up a storm. "Get me over there now, before this turns into a blood bath."

"They wouldn't--" The snow had lightened enough to spot quivers and sheaths peeking over the shoulders of the incoming skiers. Of course, they'd come armed. Briah's team hadn't left the Receiving House unarmed either, but no one was going to attack the abominables.

Briah attempted to move on her own and nearly fell. Taigan saw no choice but to help her.

The skiers reached the frantically whistling abominables before she could get Briah there. Whistling roars filled the air. The creatures were not happy, but neither were the new arrivals. The uninjured beast picked up a guard, issued an ear-piercing whistle, and flung him back towards the Temple.

At that, the soft sounds of bows being strung filled the clearing.

Shouting "no" at the others from the Temple, Briah hobbled between the groups using Taigan as a crutch.

"We're helping them. Let us finish," Briah shouted.

She held out her hands and turned back to the abominables, whistling.

The creatures whistled sharply back. Their hot breath washed over the humans. Taigan recoiled, filled again with the needs to faint and vomit. She couldn't do either now. Briah would fall atop her and, in the ensuing chaos, everyone might be slaughtered.

She took a deep breath. She could do this. She was invisible. No one cared she was here. Not even the abominables.

Briah continued to engage them, and the whistles became mournful croons.

"Help me over to him," she muttered to Taigan.

Mouth too dry to argue, she complied. She feared she might pee herself. While she fainted. Could barely breathe. She'd never been this close to a predator of any sort. She could see the individual hairs of its hide. The dirt and blood on its wickedly sharp claws. The claw on its pinky was jagged.

Briah beckoned Valene over. The group from the Temple remained frozen, arrows ready to fly.

Faster than Taigan imagined possible the remaining arrows were out of the creature, and poultices in place over all three wounds. The abominables fled, bowling over three of the new arrivals. Guards retrieved litters from the shattered Receiving House for Briah, the guard who'd been thrown, and one of the others whose leg was snapped in the creatures' flight.

Having refused to join them, she watched the skiers and injured until they reached the gates. Stepping carefully over splintered bits of wood and shards of glass, she went back inside, back into her office. Stared at her book, long forgotten by the sputtering fire.

She added a log. Realized her hands no longer shook. Gazed into the flames. A silly grin spread across her face. Had she seen what she'd done? She'd walked right up to an *abominable.* She'd been the reason Briah got there in time to prevent a massacre. She had *not* hidden under her bed. She'd faced her fears and done her part.

And now she was going to make a fresh pot of tea. And drink it with whiskey. She deserved it.

From the Second Mouth of the Mapinguari

Erik Goldsmith

I'd like the reader to believe me when I say that I've edited this three times. Only three times. I suppose you could say my first draft was abandoned however that would be the wrong word. Abandoned.

If I fix something I will *italicize* it and if I fix something a second time, it will be bold. **The question is:** *do you believe me?* Everything I'm writing is coming out as *is*, I'm not changing a word. I'm editing spelling mistakes or misplaced modifiers, but it's all coming out the way it's coming out. A word on that, if I may. I'm stuck. More precisely, I'm trapped inside a *mapinguari's stomach, which is not a* stomach at all, rather a black hole. No, not a black hole, a vortex. I don't know. I'm not a *physicist.*

My corporate body dissolved and now...*I don't* think this makes sense.

Let me start again.

I can't touch the delete button.

I do not have access to the delete button.

Let me start again.

There is *an* animal in Brazil that has lost intrigue amongst my colleagues named the mapinguari, or fetid beast. **It is or was** regarded as one of the lingering *species of* prehistoric mammals in the world, but of course, I *assumed it* was simply rumor. To be honest, the thing never interested *me* as a *subject.* I can't touch the delete *button. It demands* honesty from me. It is censoring me. It won't let me look back.

Let me start again.

Some villagers told me about it. I was doing research, I'm an anthropologist. *I was* doing research on tribal markets, inter-tribal market places...how could *I* have ever found that interesting? *They* told me to look through the trees, *past the* waterfalls. So, I did.

I found it. I found you. My lap top is still there laying on the ground. Some part of me knows that these words are being typed, populating the screen, *battery* dying.

You moved so gently. Slowly. I couldn't believe it. You looked like a giant wall of fur brushing against the trees...NO imagery. It seems I can't describe it. You are not a wall, it is a *simile...just...*no one else will understand. Let me.

My colleagues and I followed it several miles across the jungle. Slapping mosquitos from our necks, avoiding creepers, trying not to let my native friends know how winded I felt, clawing across the primordial fauna of...you were in a clearing. You were large. *You* **blocked** the sun. When you reared on your hind legs before us, more a stretch than a posture of aggression, I stared into your stomach and saw that it was not a stomach at all, but the...well, it was a hole, wasn't it? *I could see the trees on the other* side swaying in the wind, and the birds resting on branches, but the light refracted as *it came* through your belly, like I was looking through a whirlpool floating in the air. Then I

163

saw that my colleagues had run away and I was alone, transfixed by curiosity.

I refuse to say that I enjoy it. Because I don't. I can't. If you want honesty, than I can't say it.

I'm not going to say it.

From what place might I express happiness?

Not even *my thoughts*...I suppose that's all I am now... not even my thoughts can express dishonesty. I never knew how integral lying was to freedom.

In here, there is nothing to describe. I can merely describe the *flat experience I'm **having** of writing...this...I imagine* the *computer* thrown from my bag laying there in the *dirt,* wedged between root and stone. **No,** I had put it down, stopped typing, because you neared, you approached me with mammalian tenderness, and *I,* a fucking idiot. A fucking idiot. **A** fucking idiot, *reached out* and touched your nose. You swallowed me. I cannot access the delete button, because I cannot delete thoughts.

I imagine my computer sitting there, *screen open*, words **scrawling** across the white space. No fingers present. No body present.

My heart does not race, though it would. My lungs *would* crush with hyperventilation. *Tears, **tears**, would* **stream** *down my* face if I could say what I'm saying, *with* the proper voice, *the proper*...I can only panic this way...useless. Drivel.

Worthless. Spellcheck.

We walked *miles*. The natives were right. They won't come back. *Your* voice in here is *deafening*, **you** know that? Why honesty? This vortex only streams one way *forward*, what physical analogue *allows me* sentience at all?

Mapinguari.

Know one knows you exist. **Extra-terrestrial**, *immortal nonsense. A vortex* in your stomach, a mouth, what are you digesting? *No.* I don't enjoy it here. I do not.

How long have *I been in here? I can feel the computer's* battery; I feel the transference of energy. The battery is still alive. Seconds. It has taken me what seemed *centuries to* push whatever it is that I am into those *circuits. It makes* me *wonder your proximity to the* laptop. Could you still be right next to it? Have you not even turned around to return to *whatever* you call home? Why am I not dead?

You watch me muster this effort and produce each letter, caught in eternity; *am I typing* in real time beyond me, beyond you, beyond this nothingness? *Who will see it?*

No. There is no comfort in *your* company.

Leave my memories alone.
Noooapgafdubg;adfgniufnfdgauerhgenge[rgmeregmoafag. Her name is Sharon. His name is Teddy. He is my sweet boy. They are none of your concern. You don't even have the decency of language, yet you want their names.

From the Second Mouth of the Mapinguari

Fill me up. Fill me, and let this be done. You're trapped here too. Aren't you? No mate to speak of? The villagers only spoke of you. You're the female aren't you? Is this not a stomach, but *gestational sac?* **How you create** immortals. You have no answers. You have merely *membranes* of desires, limitations. Are you even asking *me* if I enjoy it here, or is that a rote *impulse* **for** *some* fetid offspring of yours? **Why** would you be able to put them back?

Ahh, I come to the futility of *questions. The battery is dying.* Will you birth me? *Anew?*

A mapinguari. Born of spaceless horror. My mother. Ravaging...eating...my memories? What is my son's name? What is my son's name? Why?

Why?

Why?

What is my wife's name? Just...No, I don't enjoy it. Please. *Who was I* trying to remember?

167

Why do you force me to show my errors? What is it you **feed on?**

Please, eat the part of me that understands. Dissolve it. The word is mercy. No I cannot be more honest.

I cannot look back. I cannot be more honest. I never knew the role lying played in freedom. I never knew the possibility of lying...had a *hand* in memory.

Language.

Yes, tear it from *me. The computer is dying.*
Tear it from me.

Tear it from me.

Hellhound

Sarah Doebereiner

Joselyn stepped as closely as possible to her mother's heels. When the woman stopped, Joselyn crashed into her backside and bounced off. She landed on the floor with an unceremonious thump that reverberated up her palms and wrists where they attempted to catch the brunt of her weight. Their neighbor, Mrs. Katie, smiled down at her.

Mrs. Katie opened a gate that partitioned the kitchen from the living room. A small stampede of puppies rushed through the space. Their tails waggled with such fervor that Joselyn wondered how they didn't fall over. The puppies reached her with their tongues in overdrive. They licked and lapped at the exposed skin on the girl's arms and legs. Her petal pink dress wrinkled where they stepped on it. She giggled.

"We'd like a male rather than a bitch," Momma told Mrs. Katie. They chatted about how the war was going and when Daddy and Mr. Katie would be home. Joselyn hoped it would be soon. She'd ask Momma what Daddy would think about them getting a dog without him. Her smile faltered then, only for a moment, before she'd answered that he wouldn't mind.

Joselyn named the puppy Lollipop because the brown and black swirls on his face reminded her of chocolate candies. Momma smiled, but it was the pinched off smile that she used sometimes when she didn't agree with Joselyn. She had said she girl could name the pup whatever she wanted, so it wasn't fair to criticize.

"We don't have to decide right away. Don't you think we should wait and see what kind of personality he has?" She asked.

Joselyn shook her head so firmly that her hair swooped into her eyes. That was the end of the conversation, for the most part. For the rest of that first day, Momma called the pup Lolli in protest. Joselyn wrinkled her nose in an attempt to mimic the woman's disapproving smile.

That night, Lolli slept on Joselyn's bed. The dog was full of life and energy during the day. They ran and played so much that they were both exhausted. Joselyn fell asleep before Momma could bring out the bedtime story she had picked.

The woman stared down at her daughter. She hoisted the puppy onto the bed next to the girl. For the first time, the puppy cried. He whimpered as though his mind had finally quieted enough to realize he was alone. He had no more mother, no more siblings, not even Mrs. Katie.

Momma rubbed the dogs head.

"Hush now. You don't want to wake her up. You're safe here."

The dog stared up at Momma with wide, frightened eyes. His nose rooted against her palm. She touched his paws absentmindedly. They were big. He would be a big, strong dog. Right now, he was just a baby, like her baby.

"You two look after each other," Momma commanded. She patted Lolli's butt. He scooted closer to Joselyn's warmth, and sucked on the girl's fingertips until he fell asleep.

The next few weeks were spent outside in the cooling, fall air. Lolli was an energetic pup who liked to chew on everything. Despite Momma's best efforts, he hadn't yet mastered the finer points of peeing outside. Joselyn and Lolli spent as much time outdoors as possible to save the furniture and Momma's sanity. When Mrs. Katie brought the remaining pups out to play, they barked at each other through the fence. The older woman spoke about the growing need for women in the workforce. Mrs. Katie knew a place, friend of a friend, if Momma was interested.

A month passed that way. Momma and Mrs. Katie met at the fence and spoke in circles of the same topics over and over. Whenever Joselyn ventured too close, they would immediately grow silent.

Joselyn threw a stick for Lolli. The pup was so excited that he ran directly into her shins and knocked the girl over. Lolli, upon hearing her cries, tried to help by jumping up and lapping his tongue all over her face. He seemed painfully oblivious that he was the one who had caused her tears in the first place. Joselyn looked for Momma, who was at her side in an instant. "Down Lolli!" Momma shouted at the dog. He put his ears back in contrition, but didn't back away. He was strong enough now that Momma had trouble moving him with only one hand. She reminded herself that that had been the point.

The worn-out brakes of a car squealed in front of the house. The flurry of movement suddenly stopped, like a record player skipping a groove. A mailman with a solemn look stepped out of the truck with a single sheet of telegram paper in his hand. Momma's eyes widened. The black pupil in their center narrowed. Joselyn stopped crying. Momma's hug tightened around her so much that it almost hurt. She had trouble catching her breath.

Lolli alone seemed unaffected by the paralyzing stillness of the moment. He growled at the mailman. His fur puffed up on ends, which made him look twice as large as he had a moment before. The skin on his lips quivered. It was the first time he had ever made such an aggressive show.

The man paused in front of the house to reread the address. He couldn't afford a heartless mistake. Momma didn't breath. She didn't respond when Joselyn spoke to her. The rapid rat tat tat of Momma's heart filled Lolli's ears. After a few moments, the man altered his approach, and walked towards Mrs. Katie's side of the fence.

Momma stood. Her voice was shaking when she spoke.

"You- ou two look after each ot-other."

Mrs. Katie wailed before the stranger handed her the letter. She sank to her knees. Momma climbed over the fence between their yards. It was something that Joselyn had never seen her mother do, nor ever would again. Time moved forward normally again. The puppies yipped along with the pitch of Mrs. Katie's sobs. Lolli stayed at Joselyn's side. He understood somehow, unconsciously, that these tears meant something different. The smell of death (faint, faraway death) lingered on the postman's letter.

Shortly after that, Momma went to work. Mrs. Katie visited while she was gone.

"It's good for her," Momma said, though Lolli never knew if she meant that it was good for Joselyn or good for Mrs. Katie. Perhaps Momma meant the two interchangeably.

Joselyn liked that Mrs. Katie let her eat sweets, run in the house, and jump on the furniture. She played the games that Momma wouldn't, and she made eggs for breakfast. Lolli always managed to secure a position to lick the plates clean as the woman washed them. It was great fun, most of the time. Only, that day, for the third day in a row, Joselyn had a fever. She hadn't been out of bed at all, and Mrs. Katie wouldn't let Lolli in with her.

He was too big she said, he would stunt her breathing.

It had started suddenly, after a trip to town. Joselyn hadn't eaten more than a spoonful of broth since. The third evening brought a chill that zapped her strength even more. By dinner time, what would normally have been dinner time, her chest hurt from coughing. Her breath was wheezy and uneven.

Sweat from Momma and Mrs. Katie made the air smell sour. Lolli watched them move through the house, trying not to get caught under their feet. He followed Momma when she went close to the door in case she wanted him.

"I'll get more medicine. I will get it. You two take care of each other," Momma spoke to Mrs. Katie.

Joselyn opened her eyes. She smiled. The medicine tasted terrible, but it didn't help ease her cough. She thought that Momma looked beautiful in the sunset light. Rouge dashed her cheeks. Her lips were red. Joselyn hadn't seen them red since Daddy left, and Lolli never had. They took it as a good omen, that things would soon be back to normal. Though tears smeared the edge of her charcoal colored eye makeup, Momma was a vision in heels as she stepped out the door.

Mrs. Katie sat quietly at Joselyn's bedside with her hands in her lap. The medicine was expensive, and they had already had their rations combined. She didn't say any of that. She didn't say anything at all in fact. Lolli watched Momma walk to the gate. He savored the scent of her perfume in the air until it was replaced with something more unnerving.

A child in a velvet dress approached the front steps. She stepped within an arm's reach of Momma on her way past. The woman didn't stop to tell the child that Joselyn was too ill to come out and play. Momma didn't pat the girls head as she went by the way she often did with neighborhood children.

Lolli watched the child's progress with cautious eyes. Despite the cold weather, her thin, frail body didn't tremor in the wind. She grasped a pinwheel in her right hand that sparkled as it spun. The stick of the pinwheel was so long that it dragged on the ground when she stepped. Lolli barked. Mrs. Katie ignored it. She didn't seem to notice the shadow creeping up the walk. Joselyn, for her part, had fallen asleep. It was a deep, unmoving sleep that felt far away from Lolli.

Lolli expected the girl to knock. He barked again to let Mrs. Katie know to expect it too. He backed away from the door and pawed at the ground. He waited for the telltale smack of her bony little knuckles against the wooden frame, but that didn't happen. The girl passed through the cherry door as if it weren't there at all. Lolli growled. Mrs. Katie was absorbed with toweling Joselyn's face.

"Be calm. I'm not your enemy," the phantom girl spoke to Lolli. The strange child smelled like the dirt after a hard rain.

The dog heard and understood the child's words. The force of her voice made his ears droop. He wanted to press his belly to the floor under the weight of her presence. He growled again. It took all the strength he had to position himself between the girl and the room beyond where Joselyn was resting.

"She can't hang on for much longer."

Lolli's voice rumbled deep inside his body. He didn't have words to give her, but she took the meaning. The girl's eyebrows pinched up in the middle. She sneered, annoyed at his lack of obedience. Or, maybe it was more than that. There was something sad tucked within the child's anger. She moved towards the bedroom.

Lolli used the last of his stamina to lunge at her. Though aiming for the girl's leg, his teeth made contact with the pinwheel instead. The wood splintered. Bits of it rolled around in his mouth and stuck in his tongue until he swallowed them, along with a burning sensation and blood.

The child cursed, surprised more than anything. A beast like that, and barely more than a whelp, shouldn't have been able to move, let alone challenge her will. Her body changed then, into something more reflective of her heavy aurora. The length of her body stretched. Long, slender limbs skeletal in their construction grew out from her chubby child's body. Her velvet dress blackened like a growing ink stain on a bit of parchment. A thick hood settled around her shoulders and shrouded her face.

The pinwheel stick grew too, thick and firm into a rod as tall as the creature. The wings folded together like a flower closing, and elongated into a single, curved blade. This was the true form of the reaper, no longer hidden to avoid frightening a child's soul. Lolli's belly hit the floor with a thud. Every hair on his body stood on end. It tickled as much as it terrified him to be so affected by the mere proximity to the creature.

"It's not my doing. The illness will take her. I'm here to protect and gather her to the world beyond. It's not my doing," the figure spoke so quietly that human hears could never have perceived it.

After a moment of thought, the tension in the creature's shoulder slumped. There was no use trying to explain it, or justify it. Such actions were a waste of time and energy. It breathed a thick sigh before drifting to Lolli's side and placing a hand on his head.

"Come with us then, if you won't be parted from her. That's all I can offer you, so you won't have to be alone in this."

The creature's touch was cold. It pulled at Lolli's core, but he refused to budge. His strength didn't leave him. His heart didn't pop open, or spill out. He sat, pinned by Death's hand, but otherwise unmoved. Rudy colored orbs peered out at him from under the hood. His own eyes shone red in response.

"Well, that – that is something different --- something I've never seen before," the creature spoke.

Lolli looked at the teeth marks on the scythe. His blood felt hot, feverish. Strength built inside him, compounded by his proximity to the scythe. If it kept up, soon he would be able to move freely again. He backed out of the creature's reach.

The shrouded figure seemed bemused by his resistance. This job, and it was a job like any other, had become so matter of fact. Blame the war, the illnesses, and the lack of resources. There wasn't time to linger on each soul like in peacetime. One fell, then another, and another without interruption until the souls all seemed alike. A child, a mother, a father at arms. It was all the same – so much so that individual countenances ceased to exist.

Yet, every once in a great while, something made Death stop. This beast, this dog, was something new. There weren't many things that could bare Death's touch without being overcome by it. It was selfish, this hesitation. Death was lagging behind schedule. How many others were suffering unduly, passed their appointed time, because of a human girl and her mutt. Death could have skipped to the next name and circled back.

There was precedence for that, especially for one so young. It was at Death's discretion. A few more days, or years, or decades. There was time for that.

Mrs. Katie cried. She tried not to for fear that if Joselyn woke the tears would frighten the child. The tears came anyway; they rolled down the crow's feet in the corners of her eyes faster than she could wipe them away.

Joselyn's breath slowed. Her spirit form rose from her still living body, barely tethered now. She looked to the hooded figure and Lolli, but felt no fear. There was a calm in even standing there that was better than the gasping, shrinking feeling of her failing lungs. It was nice to be so disconnected to her suffering body. The warmth of the dog's presence sunk into her.

"Her father is beyond already, less than a week ago. There are so many. You have no idea. She won't be alone," the reaper spoke to Lolli as if it where the worst thing that could have happened to her.

Death stretched out a hand again and touched Lolli's head. Again, the dog's spirit refused fade. It had been long since Death laid hands on something that didn't crumble in his grip. He felt the blood flowing through the animal. Its skin was soft and pliable, instead of firm or sunken. Everything he touched was too firm or rotting, everything but this. This animal was smooth and soft, without rigor or festering pieces.

Death needed to pick up the pace, to hurry up. There were many more jobs and only one of heavens ranks could field the calls. Still, just a moment more. That was okay wasn't it? Death deserved a moment's rest. Besides, if the dog was somehow beyond Death's touch, what then? He couldn't enter the realm of heavens or hells any more than Death could. Death was not allowed to step foot there, where it had already been. He couldn't follow Joselyn to the next life after all. Eventually, he would be alone.

"If I left her, would you come with me? You could go before me, herald my coming, and assist me in my work. We could..." Death stopped.

He didn't know the word for it. It was the way humans looked at each other. That thing, but Death didn't know it. Death could see it, but without know what it was. Lolli didn't respond, but the wood splinters in Lolli's belly and the power seeping into his blood resonated with Death. The energy hummed between them, more alike than different.

Death guided Joselyn back to her body, careful not to touch her. She obeyed without hesitation. Death's power over her was complete. Lolli followed close at their heels. Joselyn's spirit melted back into her body. Lolli wagged his tail, happy to see her breathing back to normal. The animosity between Death and Lolli lightened now that Joselyn was safe. He licked the tips of her fingers one last time.

"You two look after each other," Joselyn spoke, too softly for Mrs. Katie to hear.

The Corn Bear

Michael Penncavage

Like a zebra's stripe, the road cut a straight swath through the fields. Extending to the horizon in all directions the rows of corn created an endless sea of lush greens and pale yellows. A warm breeze washed over the area, causing the husks to bend in unison as they paid homage to the sun.

It was a gorgeous morning as the Pennington Peddlers Cycling Group sped along the country road. None of them could ask for better conditions. A smooth, recently paved road, infrequent hills, and a lazy, westerly wind made for ideal cycling conditions.

They had chosen this route the same way as the others – by tacking a map onto the wall and tossing a dart at it. Their monthly excursion was determined by wherever the dart landed.

It was Roger's turn this month. Having barely ever handled a dart before, the throw was awkward. The dart struck the top of the map - making his companions collectively groan. They all lived in the southern part of the state. Getting to their destination was going to be a <u>long</u> drive.

It was agreed that Roger would do some serious practice before it was his turn again.

It was late morning when the dozen riders that made up the Pennington Peddlers arrived at the Dusty Creek Motor Inn. Rick had plotted a sixty-mile course that would wind them through the countryside before placing them back at the motel.

The group got ready quickly. Bicycle gears and derailers were oiled, tires were inflated, spokes checked, water bottles filled, and by nine-thirty, the Dusty Creek Inn was a mere pinpoint in the distance behind them.

None of them had ever traveled to this part of the state before, and it was for good reason. Corn, barns, corn, cattle, corn, pigs, and more corn were the area's mainstay - a complete contrast to the more metropolitan south. Real estate was cheap and a typical farmer owned countless miles of fourth, fifth, and sixth generation land. Property lines were nonexistent, making it impossible for anyone but the owners to determine where one man's land ended and another's began.

It was a virtual sea of corn, the road parting the way as if it had become Moses, the riders the Israelites and the corn the

Red Sea.

Three hours into the ride Roger glanced at his watch. He smiled as he downshifted and pedaled harder, taking advantage of the slight decline in the road. His speedometer read 27mph and he was barely breathing hard. Earlier in the morning he had become worried about the bad throw and making everyone drive so far. But now, after they were on the road and making great time, he didn't feel as bad.

A strange rumble passed through the air. Roger glanced down at his tires, thinking that he had gotten a flat. To his relief they were fine. He turned his head so that the wind wasn't blowing in his ears and listened. He heard it again, sounding like some sort of fog-horn.

"You hear that?" he asked Stewart who pedaling by him.

"Only thing I hear is the rumble of my stomach. I'm starved!"

They passed a small, metallic sign with fading letters slightly after noon. The sign looked as if it had been peppered with buckshot years ago and never replaced. The holes punched through by the pellets were bleeding rust.

TOWN LIMITS

WOODRUFF

POPULATION: 452

A few minutes later they rode into town. Woodruff consisted of a bar, feed store, gas station, and little else. There were remnants of other abandoned buildings but they had become so weather-beaten from the bitter winters and searing summers that it was impossible to tell what they had once been.

The group stopped in front of the bar. It was so battered that it seemed like one more windstorm would be all that it needed to bring it down. A wood sign swung above the door: Jake's.

"Let's have lunch here," said Stewart as he propped his cycle against a nearby railing.

"In there?" repeated his girlfriend, Sarah, looking at him as if he were joking. "No thanks. I packed a lunch."

Stewart groaned as he pulled off his helmet and fastened it to the handlebars.

"Oats and Bananas? No thanks. I'm more in the mood for a hamburger. We've got so many miles to go that we'll burn off anything we eat, no matter how greasy it is," replied Rick as he pulled his empty bottle from its cage. "I'm out of water, anyway. If we eat in there, we can have the bartender refill our bottles."

Sarah took the lunch out from her bike bag. "Do what you want. Just don't look to me for antacids when you get start getting heartburn going up the next hill."

Once inside, it took a minute for their eyes to adjust to the bar's murky interior. The lights were on but they did nothing to reduce the gloom. The curtains were fastened so tightly over the windows that it could have been night outside. Up in the rafters, a smoke-encrusted fan slowly turned; doing little to reduce the stifling heat in the room. A pool table was in the back - the once green felt top looking as if it had not been replaced in several decades. Black-and-white photos of people dressed in long outdated clothes lined the walls. A small trophy case was off to one corner, the glass so dusty that its contents could barely be seen. A lack of tables meant dinner crowds were not a major source of revenue. It did not appear that it got much of *any* crowd since four of the barstools had their seats torn off and did not look like they were being missed.

A short, thin man who looked between 90 and 100

years old emerged through a back door, carrying a crate of beer that looked impossibly heavy for him. With surprising, ease, he hefted the crate onto the bar-top, making the bottles within clank together noisily.

"Afternoon. I'm Jake," he smiled, displaying his three stained teeth. "Hope you weren't waiting long. I was down in the cellar."

"Do you serve lunch?" asked Stewart.

Jake pondered the question as if it were one he wasn't regularly asked. "Yes. Though, we have a limited menu."

Sarah snickered and received a kick from Barney underneath the bar.

"What do you have?"

Scratching his beard, Jake thought about this for a moment. "Let's see. I could put on some cheeseburgers or hotdogs if you like. I think we have some of them buffalo wings left in the freezer."

"Anything else?" asked Sarah.

"Afraid not. Though, I got ten different beers on tap if you want something to drink," he said grinning.

They grinned back at him.

Fifteen minutes later Jake came back from the kitchen with a tray full of food. "I had some fries back there too. You sure none of you ladies would like something to eat?"

Sarah put down her glass of water. "No, thanks. I had a big breakfast."

Jake nodded as he poured another pint for Roger. "It's sure a hot one today, isn't it?"

"Yes," answered Roger's girlfriend, Laurie. She turned to Roger with a concerned look. "And *you* shouldn't be drinking so much alcohol. You're going to dehydrate."

"She's right, buddy," said Rick as he ate his burger. "We've got a lot of miles left to bike. There isn't any sag-wagon to come along and get you if you start cramping up."

Roger ignored them, finished his beer, and requested another. "Relax. There are lots of carbohydrates in beer." He looked to Stewart and grinned. "And it's common knowledge that a high carbohydrate diet is vital for people who do a lot of exercise. Besides, as long as I drink one water for each beer, I'll be fine."

A pout formed on Laurie's face. "I don't care. That's your last one."

Jake finished restocking the bar's ice chest. "Y'all are

bicyclers?"

"That's right," replied Rick. "We're touring the area for the day."

Jake leaned against the bar. "In the day I used to scoot all over this area with my bicycle. Of course that was a long time ago. Before cars were much in fashion around these parts." He cleared away the dirty dishes and placed them into the wash basin. "I trust you're all keeping clear of them Corn Bears?"

Stewart looked at him strangely. "I'm sorry…the what?"

Jake produced a towel from underneath and began wiping the bar-top. "Corn Bear, son. No one's ever told you about them?" The group gave him blank stares. Jake stopped wiping and grinned again. "Well, I reckon it's a good thing you stopped in at Jake's then."

Roger looked at the old man as if he had been doing more than just gathering bottles down in the cellar. "What exactly is a *Corn Bear*?"

"The Corn Bear is…well, I'm not really sure what it is. They live in the cornfields. Everyone who grows up in these parts knows about them."

"What do they look like?" asked Stewart, trying desperately to keep a straight face.

"Big and wide," Jake answered, using his hands to show the width.

"Cows are big and wide," said Rick.

"And they live in the corn?" asked Laurie. "What happens after the weather gets cold?"

"Legend says that it dies when the crops are harvested and is born anew with each spring thaw. Its strength comes from the crops – the higher the corn grows, the stronger and larger it gets." Jake poured himself a beer from tap. "And I can't recall a season that the corn has grown so high as this season."

"Have you ever seen one?"

"Only once. I was driving along a road not far from here when I saw something dart across the road ahead of me. It was gone in a flash and for a minute I thought it was the heat reflecting off the road, playing tricks on me. I got out of my car and walked into the grass. It had rained recently and the ground was damp. About twenty feet off the road, just inside the first row of corn, was a spot where a few of the stalks had been crushed and flattened out. Then, deep in the cornfield I heard a sound so terrible that made me jump into the truck, take off, and never look back." In one gulp, Jake drained half the mug's contents. "I always kept one eye on the cornfield after that."

"It could have been a wolf," said Rick.

"Coyotes don't venture to this area until well into the winter."

"Have these... *Corn Bears* been known to eat people?" asked Sarah, also trying to keep a straight face.

"No one's sure." Jake began filling up their water bottles from the bar's spigot. "Occasionally the police find a motorist's car off to the side of the road, abandoned."

Rick tugged on his cycling gloves. "Yeah, but that's because the serial killer probably got them."

That was cause for Sarah to hit him across his arm. "That's a horrible thing to say!"

"Okay, seriously. Maybe the car broke down and the motorist, in a fit of rage, abandoned the vehicle to the salvage yard.

"I suppose," Jake replied, scribbling out the lunch bill onto a slip of paper. "But I've always made it my policy to keep a rifle in the truck's gun rack just in case."

They passed around the bill. The five hamburgers cost a total of fifteen dollars. Sarah grinned as she waved the bill at Roger. "Hey, Roger, your beer tab was the same as all of our lunches!"

Roger looked at his empty beer glass and silently burped.

They paid the bill, left a generous tip, and headed out.

The day grew hot as the group began the return portion of the trip. The breeze, no longer at their backs, made it feel like they were now pedaling through water. The sun was unmerciful and made them drain their water bottles. Even the cars, which were usually an annoyance, had disappeared, leaving the riders alone to the road, the sun, and the wind.

And most of all, the corn.

To help fight the wind resistance they began cycling in a pace-line, the lead taking the brunt of the wind, allowing those behind to benefit from the slipstream. It helped until the wind, as if sensing it was being tricked, began to blow harder. Calves began to burn from lactic acid buildup and chests grew heavy from labored breathing. Weariness began to set in and their pace faltered. They looked for a place to take a break, to get them out of the sun, to help catch their breath, but no shade could be found. Not a tree, bush, or even a tall weed was in view to offer them refuge.

Nothing but the corn.

Roger began to slow as he coasted over to the road's

shoulder.

Rick pulled up alongside of him. "Don't tell me you have to go to the bathroom again? That's the fourth time in two hours! I told you not to drink all of those beers! You're going to shrivel up into a prune if you keep peeing as this rate."

Roger felt as if his friend might be right. Between his meager breakfast and the beers, his legs had become leaden sinkers, his mouth a cotton factory, and his lips dried worms. "Don't worry. I'll catch up," he said, walking through the first row.

The corn towered above him and the stalks grew so thick that they felt like prison bars. The farmer had planted the seeds in straight lines, perfectly spaced, making the corn stalks look like soldiers in perfect formation.

Roger walked in deep, making sure that a passing motorist, or worse, a cop wouldn't see him. He wasn't sure if it was a fining offense, but knowing his luck, it probably was.

The immense corn leaves, eager to absorb as much of the sun as possible, created a natural canopy. As a result, most of the rays did not reach the ground, which made the air cool and the ground moist.

Finishing his business, Roger closed his eyes and leaned

against a stalk, grateful that it was able to support his weight. The air's moisture and coolness felt refreshing. He dreaded going back out into the sun…

A sudden rustling broke the silence. Roger opened his eyes and was roused from his daze as he tried to determine which direction it had come from. The rustling happened again and he looked to his left…

He let out a sigh of relief. *Just the wind blowing through the leaves.* A bead of sweat dribbled down his forehead and off his nose. Jake's tall tales were playing tricks with his mind. He turned quickly and strode through the corn towards the road.

However, after a dozen rows, he hadn't reached the road. Roger retraced his steps. Pushing aside the stalks, he walked back through the rows, looking for the marker he had left. However, after walking the same distance, he did not come across the puddle.

Panic seized him.

He was lost.

Roger cursed himself for being so careless. Every moment he spent wandering around, his friends were slowly distancing themselves from him.

He tried listening for sounds of passing cars to help him

find the right direction. All that he heard was his rapid breathing and his heart pounding in his ears.

He began walking, certain he was now going in the right direction. *Perhaps I walked farther into the field than I thought.* With each step his bicycle shoes sank deep into the mud, making a sucking noise as he yanked them out.

The same fog-horn sound from before reverberated through the air. It was louder than before and seemed so out of place that it began to make Roger nervous.

The approaching roar of a car engine made his heart skip a beat. *The road.* He was heading in the right direction. Roger ran faster, not bothering to push aside the stalks. The corn battered and cut him as he stormed through. Roger felt a trickle, which he knew wasn't sweat, run down his temple

Through the vegetation Roger caught a glimpse of something metallic. *The bicycle.* He saw the black shimmer of the road through the stalks. He was almost there.

Something snagged his ankle. He spun around to keep his balance. His momentum propelled him out of the corn and into the grassy shoulder that separated the field from the road.

The corn rustled and shook violently behind Roger. The air grew foul. Roger glanced over his shoulder. After a moment he realized that whatever was within the corn was not venturing any closer. Either it couldn't or wouldn't venture out into the sunlight. The cornfield, as immense as it was, was its prison.

Roger sighed in relief.

He had escaped.

Roger turned to pick up his bicycle when he heard a shuffling of feet up by the roadside. He squinted and saw Jake approaching. A shotgun was slung over his shoulder. "Get yourself into a bit of trouble, there?" he said. "Damn, you look worse than a fellow I once saw attacked by a Doberman."

"It's…right there… inside the corn," Roger gasped, pointing.

Jake looked past him and into the field.

Roger took a step forward. Jake leveled the shotgun at him. He stopped short and impulsively backtracked. "What the hell are you doing?"

"Did I or did I not warn you to stay out of the cornfields?"

"It…I had to go to the…" Roger lost his train of thought as he stared at the shotgun. The wounds caused by the corn were excruciating.

Jake spat onto the ground. "You go running into the

field, excite my babies, make them think it's feeding time and then decide to just run away? Don't you think that's a little unfair?"

The corn began to rustle again. The air became even more foul than before. Roger felt a shadow rise behind him and realized he had taken too many steps backwards.

Jake watched as Roger was pulled through the stalks. A short, pathetic scream sounded. Jake watched the tops of the corn stalks began to sway as the Corn Bear quickly took its prey deep within the field.

Silence followed.

Jake threw his shotgun behind the bench. He looked up and down the road.

Not a car was in sight.

Jake hoisted himself into the cab, hit the ignition, and drove off.

In the weeds, Roger's bicycle still lay - its rear wheel spinning freely in the warm summer air.

Spring-heeled Jack: The Terror of London

Nemma Wollenfang

Whitechapel, 1838

"It was him, I swear it!" exclaimed the young swain, all wide-eyed and flustered, with his hair in a state of abject disarray and the cravat at his throat untied. "With claws curved like talons an' eyes like great blazing balls o' fire! Leapt clear across three building, he did!"

The tankard in his grip visibly shook; Jack could see it from three tables away. The amber brew within sloshed over the sides, splattering the table he and his three companions shared in the centre of the public house – all of whom were clearly of a disbelieving nature.

"Someone's been swilling the old rotgut," the more portly one chuckled.

"Had a tad *too* much by the sounds of it too," chortled the reed-thin second, sharing a semi-amused, semi-concerned look with the first, clearly questioning the youth's sanity.

199

But the poor lad looked pale as death; ashen of cheek and white of lip, and he shook his head at their attempts at good cheer. "No," he said, with a most macabre tone. "It ain't that. I don't care what ya say. No amount o' gin nor opiates could make me see such a heinous thing. Diabolical, it was! Old Springheel. I won't ever forget it, no matter how long I live…"

Excitable youth. Not that Jack could blame him. Many such grew insensible at the sight of him – his real, unveiled self that was. Some grew nigh deranged, becoming a hindrance to their families. Others earnt themselves a cot at Bedlam. Papers had seen fit to record his more Machiavellian misdeeds too, making them common knowledge, as was the fashion of this era. That only incited greater hysteria among the populace, more exaggerated sightings. Tales passed more swiftly now than they ever had in older times. This was a new and interesting trend for Jack. It meant their fear spread that much faster as well, like wildfire.

Yet still, none here realised that very same villain sat amongst them, a fox in a hen coop. Jack chuckled to himself in the far corner, taking a hefty swig of his own ale. Mere dregs remained. Not that it mattered; the pewter flagon was only for show, a mere prop to explain away his presence in the smoky

establishment… while he perused what stock there was available:
a barmaid with a prodigious bosom and a wealth of frizzy
copper hair who served the patrons with a gap-toothed smile, a
pox-ridden waif of no more than a dozen years that sat peeling
potatoes in a corner, and a haggard fishwife whose husband had a
roving eye. His stomach growled, beyond famished. He must eat
soon. Yet none here tickled his fancy.

It was a dark, seedy, little tavern, tucked into a dank
corner of Whitechapel. It was the kind of place where ale was
cheap, the women cheaper, and, if one knew whom to approach,
so was a sticky little ball of oblivion from an opium monger. The
choking air stunk of burning cheroot and the only illumination
came from the merrily crackling hearth over the far side of the
room, leaving all else cloaked in shadow. This suited Jack best,
made it easier to hunt.

"You've been reading too many sightings, gotten yourself
spooked, lad," the oldest of the three finally said, a man with an
abundance of wrinkles and hair as white as salt. "No wonder.
The papers have turned crazed with this newest spate of 'Spring-
heeled Jack' stories. Why, I even read one report myself just
this morning which again made claim to the metallic claws, but
also stated that he vomited out blue and white flames! Ha! The

absurdity!"

The youth nodded, swallowing hard as he examined the scars in the woodgrain before him. "Aye, that report. Did you also read what he did to that girl? Clawed to shreds, it said."

By the silence that came after, he likely had. Their company grew solemn then, silent, each seeing to his own tankard with not a word more shared between them, all affected by the dour mood of the one. Not long after they fetched up their frock coats and top-hats to make their departure.

Think I'll take my leave too, Jack mused. *Since there's nothing here to my taste.*

Like a shadow he trailed the men, out into the mizzling rain. Light, mere drizzle, but it was enough to make them hunch in upon themselves and pay less heed to their surroundings. To him. None noticed that a fifth trailed their party. Why Jack did it, he did not know. Boredom, perhaps. Or mayhap he was still a little intrigued by the frightened youth. It was not often he came across one so clearly affected by the sight of him as he leapt about on his nightly wanderings, from rooftop to rooftop. And that a mere glimpse, from a distance, had debilitated the boy in such a way, destroying his peace of mind when he had not even an assault to claim…well, it amused him. Had his reputation truly grown so strong?

Carriages rolled along the cobblestone streets: landaus and phaetons, curricles and barouches. Some led by a single horse and a scraggly driver, others driven by teams of high-stepping stallions of immaculate grooming and footmen in pristine regalia in the colours of their households. All heading home before the night deepened any further.

Some contained females of a fairer nature than Whitechapel's gutters could offer, their perfume catching in his nostrils as it twirled on the breeze. But 'twould do little good to attempt to assail them in so public a place. And besides, he'd not fared well with carriages in the past. Jack kept on the group, a distance away but not so far as to miss their chatter.

"Try to put it from your mind, dear boy," the oldest was saying to the dishevelled youth. "Focus on other matters."

The boy shook his head. "I'll only rest easy again when these attacks abate, the reports disperse. Until then worry will plague me for my sweet Nancy. I could not abide any bad thing befalling her, she's just so sweet and innocent, and she means *everything* to me!"

"Well, at least there's one thing," the portly one said, clapping him upon the shoulder, "the beast has only been known to attack at night, most often in the suburbs. She lives all the way over in Mayfair in that fancy house, and she wouldn't dream o' wandering at night."

The youth perked up a little. "Aye, 'tis true. Nancy will be safe in her home for sure. Her papa's right protective too. No need to fret on that account."

Not long after that the comrades dispersed, each heading in his own direction, and, as he watched the last of their frock tails disappearing around a far corner, Jack was once again left alone. A deep rumble churned his gut. Now was the time. Night was his hunting ground, smog-laden London his domain. The hour had grown late, the streets mostly empty. A man on a penny farthing rolled by and a trio of ragged-looking workmen braved one of the region's more salacious establishments. At one corner a lonely whore in a dirty red dress solicited services.

"Three penny upright, sir?" she called out as he passed.

Hmm, the girl was young and appealing. Street-walkers were easy. Out roaming the late hours, unprotected, alone. Nobody missed them. Nobody even noticed when they were gone. The papers were yet to account for them while tracking his many misdeeds. Already he had sampled many of their lower ilk – the blondes, the brunettes, the red-heads. Skin of all shades.

But his palate craved different game tonight. Something fresh and refined and lovely.

Something pure.

Or mayhap something beloved…

"Nancy…" The name of that unkempt youth's sweetheart rolled around on his tongue like so many dark pearls. *The girl he thought to be safe…*

If he were to track her, what a wicked joke that would be.

But how to go about it? He had no scent, no likeness, no address to follow.

Only a name.

The boy! *He* knew. And… as Jack lifted his head, nostrils flaring… Yes! He was not so far away. Still within reach. Taking to a nearby alley, Jack used the hard metal of his claws to scale the brick of the building, making short work of the ascent until he stood atop, sniffing again. West, the boy was heading west. He took the buildings one leap at a time, over and again, barely alighting upon one set of slate tiles before he leapt to another, until he was hovering on a gable just above where the youth walked. Alone now. It was almost too easy.

In a flap of black, his cloak billowing about him like a pair of giant membranous wings, he landed upon the pavement at the boy's feet with all the grace of a feline.

Wide, white eyes greeted him. Brimming with fear. His mouth opened, about to shout. But Jack was quick, and in a flash of movement he had the boy by the throat pressed up against a red brick wall in the nearest alley. As he scrabbled, hands clawing against his hold, Jack allowed his carefully erected visage to crumble, letting the youth witness the full horror of his true image – the one he hid while mingling amongst civilised society.

Eyes burning like hellfire, skin as flawless and silver as steel, jagged horns sprouting from a mess of black hair. A mouth that opened to spew torrents of white and blue flame… Just as his friend had described. A tad excessive, even Jack had to admit, but he did so like to see the poor humans quail. This one, it appeared, was beyond even the capacity to scream.

"Where is this girl of yours?" he grated, voice scraping like nails. "Where is Nancy?"

Something like sanity returned to his bulging eyes; a wrath that battled against the all-consuming fear, and, surprisingly, won.

"Don't you dare lay a hand on her, ya filthy-"

"Ah!" Jack squeezed his throat until the boy choked on

his curse. "Language."

He could not abide a foul tongue – they tasted so coarse.

"Now, let's try that again."

"I'll never tell! Would rather die!"

With great pomp, Jack raised his serrated iron claws to buff on his lapels, making sure they caught the waning light of the moon. From the boy's gulp, he was sure they did.

"I ask again, where is…"

It was then, as the boy struggled, that a golden locket slipped loose from his shirt front, dangling between them like an offering. Ah, did sweethearts not use these? To harbour the likeness of one another while parted? With a smile he lifted it up, and against his other hand the boy struggled in earnest.

"Don't… don't…" Jack flicked it open. Inside, lay the image of a wondrously handsome creature. Skin pale as porcelain, gleaming hair as golden as corn.

And, encased in the window beside it, a lock of hair. Her scent.

"Perfect. That's all I need."

"NO!" The boy choked, reaching. But Jack was already gone, scaling the building and leaving the red-faced swain coughing on his hands and knees.

Her scent was all he needed. Now he had it, the hunt would be easy. His senses had become so finely attuned over the centuries that it would likely take little work to track it.

From one building to another he leapt, scenting the air. Again, again…

When Big Ben tolled the hour he caught a hopeful whiff – floral, freesias and roses. Was it… yes. His Nancy.

It led to the rich quarter, to a fine five-storey Mayfair manor of white brick, with thin Roman columns and tiny balconies flanking the upper floors. He took the fence in one silent leap, and from the shadows of its leafy garden he watched. Around him the chatter of insects died and the shrubs grew silent; the smaller creatures recognising the ancient predator in their midst. The girl sat at a vanity on the third floor, combing out her long golden tresses, dressed only in a thin linen nightshift. Rosebud lips, porcelain skin, a cherub's dimples. She could be no more than sixteen – the sweetest of ages. And as he watched, her maid bade her goodnight and left her alone. Perfect. With a swish of his hand, Jack altered his appearance once again – presenting the misleading visage of a handsome rake, not the iron-skinned monstrosity he truly was. Most suspected his true nature, instinct warned them well, but it hurt naught to try. Then, without a sound, he hopped up onto her balcony, as sleek as any alley cat, and stepped towards her bedchamber. The open doors beckoned like an open pair of arms, the flimsy gossamer of their long curtains billowing out into the night-

Argh! The burn!

Teeth bared he reeled back, his façade flickering. Blasted wardings. The outer walls were riddled with them. Cherokee charms, Vatican relics, symbolic repellents etched into the brick. Talismans and enchantments of every conceivable sort. *Tricky, tricky...* The wealthy young mothers of Mayfair may not be so wise to his ways, but the older women were – those who remembered the unreported raids of their youths, when he had indulged a good twenty years back and taken three dozen maids to feed his hunger – and apparently they had grown canny in their protections. Likely due to the recent reports. But Old Jack was canny too, and devious, all the more for his five hundred years. He knew ways around them.

He shifted slightly, careful not to get too close, examining the wards from every angle. They shimmered like amethyst, hovering just shy of the bricks in a misty hue invisible to human eyes. These were potent indeed, powerful markings; the family must be rich to afford such protections. And, to his immense frustration there was simply no way to bypass them. They were far too strong. He would not cross this threshold. But... that meant nothing. There were always ways around such things. He would just have to conduct this hunt *differently*.

She must come to *him*. And that could easily be accomplished.

Controlling his visage he leant back against its rail, and clearing his throat he called out. "Greetings, sweet girl." Masking the gravel of his voice, he used his most alluring tone.

One which rarely failed.

"Oh!" She startled, spinning around on her little stool. For a moment she simply stared, like a rabbit facing a fox. Then she blinked. "Sir... What are you doing all the way up here?"

No fear, mere surprise. How refreshing. Like a new hatchling she knew not to be afraid.

No wonder the boy had been so afraid for her.

"Forgive me," he said, affecting a contrite demeanour. "When I saw you from the street I could not help myself. I simply had to climb up here and meet such an exquisite beauty."

The flattery called forth a rosy red blush. Ah, so young, so inexperienced...

Shy she dipped her head. "I do not usually entertain gentleman callers at this late hour."

Her uncertainty incited a wicked smirk. Of course she did not, the girl reeked of purity. That was what had drawn him.

"Fear not. I mean only to steal a kiss, and your heart." He grinned winningly.

A smile blossomed, as bright as her blush. "I think you are a rogue, sir!"

"Likely so." He added a devilish wink that inspired the sweetest little chuckle and made the pink in her cheeks deepen to rouge.

Seeming to recall herself, the girl grew contrite, hands folding in her lap. "Besides, I have a beau, sir, a good man who says he loves me dearly."

"Ah, 'tis no surprise, a girl as fair as you." Jack shook his head, as if he thought himself a fool for hoping. "Dismiss me then and I shall not trouble you again."

Using a heartsick sigh he'd perfected over the ages, he twisted on the rail and made as if to jump back down into the fragrant shrubs of the garden.

"Wait!" Her hand reached out – as he'd hoped – and she stood, stepping closer. His muscles tensed at her approach, at her proximity, at her floral perfume. *Just a little closer…*

Then, in the demurest of voices, she asked, "A kiss?"

Predictable as the changing tides. They always fell for a Devil's charm.

With one crooked finger he coaxed her forward. "Come out onto the balcony, sweet girl. Step into the moonlight." *Where there's no talisman to protect you.*

Compulsion throbbed through her, he felt it, provoked it, drawing her beyond her home's protections. And as soon as she stepped outside, he swept her into his arms. Like a spider with a moth, he had her ensnared in his silken embrace. Up close, her sweet scent was all the more intoxicating. Ah, it had been some time since he'd found such lovely prey.

"Close your eyes," he bid.

Lips pursed, head tilted back, she did as he bid.

This girl had been protected too well. Sheltered to a harmful degree. Someone should have warned her, this was not even sporting. But he was not about to give up his prize.

And such a pretty prize she was.

Lifting a hand, he caressed her cheek with the backs of his fingers. So soft, so silky. Under his touch she shivered. His hand trailed down and down, until it lay upon her chest.

Where the beat hummed strongest.

There, he allowed his hand to turn. In a flash, he struck. Talons dug deep. Flesh and bone caved to them like butter. Then he felt it, that fluttery rhythmic pulsing. Her heart.

A second was all it took; a second was all she felt. A soft breath, a gasp of peppermint, and the girl-child slumped in his arms. In one hand, dripping red pulp, lay his grisly prize.

He held it close while he cradled her body – the sweet, fluttery thing that may sate his hunger for decades to come. Then, with care, he lay the fair maid down upon the balcony. They would find her come dawn, looking so serene, so peaceful she might be sleeping.

Far to the east, muted by distance, Jack could just make out the frantic tramp of feet – the kind that came with a person running. Along with a breathless, repetitive gasp.

"Nancy... No, Nancy..."

The young swain was too late.

Jack smiled a little as he looked down upon the fair maid. Then, with tender regard, he placed a kiss upon her cooling lips.

Old Springheel was, after all, a man of his word.

The Keystone State

Paul Stansfield

"So anyway, the theory is that the whole movie is in Cameron's head, what he imagines it would be like to be a popular kid's friend, and…." She noticed Ray wasn't walking with her. Simone turned around. He was back about fifty feet, kneeling near a big tree off the hiking path.

"What are you doing?" He continued staring down. Simone saw there was a large hole near the base of the tree. Finally Ray looked up.

"What? Oh, sorry. This is a hemlock tree. And we're near a still pond. And there's a big burrow-looking hole here. So I stopped." He smiled at her puzzled look. "Remember? The squonk."

"Right. The crying one. I liked that story. Sort of a bizarre non-sequitur beastie. But why are you stopping here?"

"Because. It's like the story goes. I want to check it out." His voice was taking on a higher pitch, as it often did when he was getting agitated.

Simone forced herself to take a deep breath. Then another. "It's a fun little book. About folklore. Some of the other stories were about the hoop snake, and the hide-behind, and that goat like thing which had legs shorter on one side so it could run around mountain tops better."

"Yes! I know. But there's often a kernel of truth underneath the folklore. And remember my great uncle's story. I'm not saying it's real, but maybe, just maybe, there's something to it."

"The same guy who thought that Jimmy Carter was behind the JFK assassination? And that the Nazca Lines were alien runways?"

He turned back to the tree, and the hole. "Yes. Later he got senile, or whatever. But the story in question was when he was young. Look, go on ahead. I'll catch up with you. I haven't meditated yet, so if nothing else, I'll get that in."

Simone started to speak, then managed to stop herself.

She took some more deep breaths. "Fine. I'll see you in a bit."

She resumed walking. The trail made several turns as it wound its way through the forest. It was nice to get outdoors again, to feel fresh air instead of the canned, temperature-controlled air of the office. To see trees, and rocks, and dirt instead of the painted cinder block walls, and cubicles. Walking on the treadmill kept her in shape, but walking outside was way more interesting. Periodically she would stop for a moment, and wait. Sure enough, usually an animal would come into view with each little bit of quiet. A squirrel, a cute looking chipmunk, and a red-tailed hawk, high in a tree.

But Ray didn't catch up. She rounded a final bend, and there he was, still by that tree. In a familiar pose. Kneeling, arms outstretched, eyes closed. Muttering quietly— probably a chant. She walked up silently, and sat down near him.

After a moment she zoned out. Thoughts about work projects, television shows, and hockey flicked through her mind. Ray's hand on her shoulder almost caused her to yell.

"Don't move. Or speak. It's coming out."

She started to say something sarcastic, but then she

heard something. A throaty vibration. A scraping sound. Shit, something was coming out. She started to stand up, but Ray's grip on her shoulder tightened, and kept her down.

A thing came out of the hole. She gaped at it. It looked formless, like a black garbage bag. But no, she saw, that was its skin: dark gray, wrinkled, and loose, like a Shar-Pei's, only bigger, uglier. Odd, irregular bumps dotted its hide. A smaller protrusion (the head?) was at the front. Slowly it came up to Ray. After a long pause, a part of it rose up. A paw—it had fingers almost like claws or something. She gasped as this foot was gripped in Ray's left hand, while his right stayed on her shoulder.

Simone stared. As she peered closer, she could make out a face of sorts on the head. Sunken, beady eyes. A snout-like projection. She could feel some sweat trickling down her back. She wanted to speak out, to pull away. But she couldn't.

Finally, after ten minutes or more, the thing let go of Ray's hand. It shuffled backwards, back in the hole. After it was gone Ray removed his hand from her shoulder.

"Guess my Uncle Otto wasn't entirely crazy, huh?" He stood up, and helped Simone stand, too. She felt a little shaky.

He started walking back toward their rental cabin. "C'mon, I have quite a story to tell."

Her eyes flicked nervously back at the hole. She couldn't see anything in it. She followed after Ray.

"Alright, we've eaten, now tell me what the fuck that was." She pushed her plate away, and leaned back in her chair.

"Okay, fair enough. I wanted to mull it over for a while. And I love being dramatic, as you know." Simone touched her nose with her index finger in an exaggerated fashion. "I started by calming myself. Losing myself, in a way. Getting in touch with nature, so to speak. Then I reached out, with peaceful, supportive thoughts and emotions. It was like in my class, with---ah, never mind. You saw the result. Gradually I sensed something was there, receiving me. And gradually its feelings and emotions were communicated to me. Stronger and stronger. Then after it came out, and we made bodily contact it grew incredibly more powerful still. We connected in real, profound way."

"So what is it, then? What's the deal?"

"It's what we heard. A squonk. Well, I doubt they call

themselves that, but it's the creature we read about, heard about. It's hard to describe. We didn't talk back and forth, like people, but we communicated all the same. I....saw things in my head, images and stuff, and did the same thing back to it. It's a weird animal. It has a symbiotic relationship with the hemlock tree. It lives near their roots, and feeds off the dirt around them. Some micro-nutrients, or something. And its waste in turn helps fertilize the tree. But the most important thing is—the stories were right. They're fucked up, mentally. I've never felt so much self-loathing. They're hideous, and THEY KNOW IT. It's deeply ashamed, to a ridiculous degree. The other details are right, too. If you corner one, it will dissolve into a liquid. Not tears, exactly, though. But somehow they can re-solidify again. Somehow. I'll learn more about that, and other things."

"You're going to communicate with that....thing again?"

"Yes, of course. Where's your sense of scientific curiosity? It's a new creature. Folklore that's real. If we stumbled upon a Bigfoot, wouldn't you want to learn about it?"

"I guess. It's just....it makes me nervous somehow. It's so weird."

"I know. I know. It's just because it's different, and new. You'll get used to it. So will I." Ray stood up. "All this mind melding has made me tired. I'm gonna take a nap. Wake me up at like nine, please." He went into the bedroom, and then into bed. Within a minute or two he was breathing heavily, obviously asleep. That never ceased to annoy Simone. It made her jealous, since it took her 15-30 minutes to fall asleep, sometimes longer.

But no matter. There were more important things to consider now. She found the book of folklore, opened to the relevant pages, and reread about the creature. Then she opened up her laptop, and looked up everything she could about it, all the folk tales and local legends. Most of it was pretty much the same. All absurd, really. This thing couldn't be more laughable, or pathetic.

Despite this, she kept shivering.

Once again, he spent practically all day with Terry, as he'd named it. He said its name for itself was an unpronounceable string of noises and concepts. And then, as before, he spent much of the night writing pages in his notebook, "while his thoughts and feelings were still fresh." And after that, mostly what he wanted to talk about was Terry, and "squonk history." It was amazing how quickly Simone had gotten bored with this. She liked animal facts as much as the next person, but it was too much. But when she complained, said how they were wasting much of their precious two weeks of vacation for this year, Ray would get defensive and snappy. He accused her of being selfish. It was an enormous scientific breakthrough and all. He was helping a psychologically damaged entity, too. Already he was seeing improvement in its mood, and attitude. He was hopeful that eventually it would agree to be seen by others. And then Ray could quit his computer programming job and do what he really wanted to do—help animals, explore the mind and metaphysics, and probably get wealthy and famous to boot.

And all of that was true, to an extent. It was incredible that this animal was real, and it was cool to learn about it. Plus, she knew that Ray only did programming to pay the bills, and because he had some talent at it, but he didn't feel passion for it. Obviously she wanted him to be happy. But it was all too much. She needed some attention too. This was all so sudden, so overwhelming. She'd basically spent a week by herself. And the actual animal bothered her. She'd gotten used to it, a little, and had even touched it. She could feel pity for it, since it was so miserable and unhappy. But it was so weird. Not like a snake, or a spider, or a rat—its own thing, bizarre. Disquieting. She couldn't put her finger on it, but something about it creeped her out, and not because it was physically ugly, either.

At least they were still having regular sex. If Simone's emotional needs weren't being met, at least her physical needs were. During these times Ray was attentive, and thorough. After their bout that night she threw him a bone, and actually brought up Terry and squonks herself.

"So you said squonks have a strange reproductive process, right? No sex?"

"Right. Asexual reproduction. Which is good—because with their depression otherwise they'd never seek each other out! It's like an amoeba or something. They produce buds, which grow into other squonks. But of course because of their terrible outlook on life, they're not motivated to do it that much. So, that, among other things, is why they're so rare. Terry did indicate that baby squonks grow up pretty quick, though."

"How many are there, anyway? How come no one but your great uncle, and a few others, ever encountered one?"

"Their shyness, for one. They can sense people, and stay in their holes when we're around. Plus they move around on the ground mostly at night. And it's hard to get a handle on how many there are. They don't visit with each other much. They're pretty solitary. So I think there's probably only hundreds total. And the gypsy moths and that sap-sucking insect are playing havoc with their habitat, destroying the hemlocks they need to live."

Simone turned over. "Okay, they're rare, and live in heavy woods, and they're shy, and all. But it's like the Bigfoot problem. Even with all that, how come no one ever found a dead body, or bones?"

"That's easy. They dissolve, remember? When they expire they liquefy. That's funny, too. Terry communicated how predators sometimes attack them. Bobcats, foxes, and bears. Sometimes they surprise a squonk and even bite into one. But then it instantly turns to liquid. It's one of the few lighter moments I've gotten from Terry. Apparently even a clinically depressed animal finds it amusing when a bear or fox is suddenly

astonished, and puzzled. But Terry's getting better. I think its
mood has gone from near-suicidal to just very pessimistic.
Terry's getting more communicative every day. I'm hopeful
that it'll agree to other people seeing it. Which would be great.
What a discovery! It'll be on the cover of Nature and National
Geographic for sure. I—well, we, sorry, will be rolling in it. And
then I'll…." He stopped. He nudged Simone gently. She didn't
reply. He chuckled to himself and rolled over. Within a minute
or two he was also asleep.

"Will it stain the rug?" asked Simone.

"No. Well, I don't think so. How could it? It'll all turn
back solid. But shhhh, let's watch."

The squonk shuffled around for a moment. Simone even
caught a glimpse of its feet, underneath its loose, baglike skin.

Then it collapsed, with frightening speed. She gasped.
A large puddle of grayish-black liquid was now in its place. She
took a step back from it. A look at Ray showed he was writing
furiously in his notebook. He'd wanted to film it with his phone,
but Terry had nixed that, strongly. Ray was already treading
on thin ice with it. It had taken all his emotional support and

cajoling to get it to come inside the cabin.

The liquid moved around a bit, roiling its surface. Then in a flash it was gone, in barely a blur. And then the squonk was back solid again. Ray laughed, and clapped. After a beat, Simone did, too. Ray approached, and bent down, extending his hand. Terry obligingly stuck out its forepaw, looking for a moment like a pet dog. A pretty hideous dog, but one all the same. The room grew quiet as they linked up.

After a few minutes Simone went over to the couch and sat down. She sighed, and picked up the Janet Evanovich paperback she was reading. Ray spoke up after she'd read about twenty pages.

"Okay, Terry's had enough of inside. We're going outside for a few hours. Back at six." He opened the door, and waited for Terry to shuffle through. Then he went through himself, closing the door behind him as Simone mumbled a "Bye."

She'd finished the book, and gotten dinner ready before Ray returned. Not that the latter had taken long. There was plenty of pizza left over, and the microwave heated it up rapidly. They ate in silence—Ray with his left hand, while his right wrote copiously in his notebook. Simone finished her dinner, and then caught a couple of episodes of "Breaking Bad" on her computer. Then Ray finally joined her on the couch.

"What did you learn today?"

"A lot more about their social lives. Or really, the lack thereof. They can communicate with each other over quite the distance. Somewhat. Like with me, it's more detailed when they have physical contact with each other. It's hard to explain."

"Is it like the Borg—a hive mind?"

"No, not as far as I can tell. It's like yelling over a long distance. But they're individuals. I think." He chuckled. "They're so weird! It can take forever to get across simple concepts. Since the communicating isn't really with words. Not like us, anyway. But Terry's getting so much better. It even made a jokey remark today. Sort of. It told me I was ugly. I know, it won't be doing an HBO standup special anytime soon, but it's a big step for it. Its mood is so much healthier. Night and day."

"Has Terry agreed to come with us in a couple days?"

Ray's face fell. "Not sure. I mentioned how there's a woods nearby. Which I think has some hemlocks. But it's reluctant. It's still afraid of people. So much. I'm still working on it. I've communicated how we live far away, and can't just drive out here and back repeatedly. I don't know—we'll see."

"Did you tell anybody about it, finally?"

"No, not yet. Nobody's gonna believe me unless it's sitting there right in front of their eyes. So that'll have to wait, too."

Hours later, there was movement beside the hole by the big hemlock. Several grayish-black shapes moved together under the dim moonlight. Just before dawn they broke apart.

Simone woke up and groaned. She was about two minutes from pissing herself, it felt like. She shoved the covers aside and got up, and then padded to the bathroom.

As she sat there, feeling it pour out of her, she sniffed. I'm getting old, she thought. Seems like I can't sleep through an entire night without a pee break these days.

Finished, she stood up and started to flush. Then stopped. Ray was a pretty heavy sleeper, but there were limits. And this bathroom was much closer to the bed than the one in their apartment back in Wilkes-Barre. Instead she left it to mellow, as the saying went, and washed her hands quickly.

She was just about to snap off the light when movement caught her eye. Ray's upper body was illuminated by the bathroom light. She walked over a few feet. Yes, there, by his face. Grayish liquid was pouring into his ears, nose, and mouth. He started to cough and snort at the same time.

She started to walk over to him when she found herself on the floor, ears ringing from the roar. She was dizzy, and..... wet? She rubbed at her face, and it came away bloody. But not from her—she checked. Something was stuck to her forehead. She raked at it. It was a chunk of skin, with black hair on it.

Simone struggled to her feet and looked at Ray. Terry was sitting on top of him. Then the squonk moved over, and she saw Ray's head was gone. She looked around. Blood and small pieces of flesh and bone were everywhere. Terry moved toward her, and this broke her paralysis. In an instant she was through the doorway, and into the living room, with the door shut behind her. Her heart pounded in her ears as she searched for the car keys. Then her purse. Her eyes flickered to the door. A grayish-black liquid was seeping underneath the tiny crack at its base. She saw Ray's notebook and stuffed it into the top of her purse.

Then she was out the door, slamming it shut behind her. Not that this would do much. She dropped the keys in her haste, picked them up, and opened the car door, turned on the ignition. Just before she backed up she could see the liquid squonk flowing across the front porch.

After she'd gone about ten miles, she stopped at a gas station. Surely it couldn't move that fast, right? Her hands were shaking so much that she had to use both, and several tries at that, to get her credit card into the reading slot. While it was filling she looked in the back. Her hiking backpack was there. An old pair of sweat pants and a sweatshirt were promptly pulled on over her light t-shirt and boxer shorts. That was something.

She pushed "9" on her cell phone, and then paused. What could she say? An obscure mythological beast is real, and exploded my boyfriend? With the only physical evidence being scribblings in a notebook, and her word? Fuck, they didn't even have shitty cell phone video or pictures of this thing. She put the phone back in her purse. No, she'd be arrested, and/or committed. She had to think.

The tank was full. She replaced the pump in its holder, and got back into the driver's seat. A look at the road behind her showed nothing flowing up its surface. But for how long?

Simone pulled out of the gas station lot, and onto the road. She forced herself to stay at the speed limit this time. She thought about buying some coffee, or an energy drink, but then dismissed this idea. She was already wired enough as it was, even if it was a four hour drive.

She needed to think.

Simone paused for a brief moment, then typed, "Believe me, I know how this all sounds. But look at the facts. You'll find no evidence of an explosive, or fragments of shotgun pellets, or anything like that in the cabin. This isn't the movie Scanners, people's heads don't blow up like that on their own, no matter how strong a stroke they have. I'm willing to get a psychiatric evaluation, but PLEASE try to keep an open mind, and check out what I'm saying, seriously." She hit return, and then wrote," Sincerely, Simone L. Oldham." She scrolled back up and checked the whole email. Then the address line, and who she'd cc'ed. Four other friends, the FBI, and the local police for the cabin. This email had taken forever. God, this computer was slow! Which made sense, since it was so old. She was glad she was lazy, and hadn't gotten around to throwing it out yet. She guessed her new laptop would be in the police evidence room soon.

She glanced up, and blanched. The window above her head was shut, of course, but a thin line of grayish black liquid was seeping through underneath. Simone hit "send" just as the liquid already on the computer's backside poured in. The screen went dark, and sparks flew. A small electric fire started, accompanied by black smoke.

Simone was already at the door, when she saw a familiar sight underneath it. She turned to the window over the fire escape, and saw more of the same. A glance at her desk revealed that her cell phone was already inundated underneath its own pool of grayish black liquid, and smoking as well. Trembling, she went the only place she could, back into the corner of the living room.

The liquid just got deeper. Gallons, flowing toward her. How many were there? This couldn't just be Terry. And how had they traveled here so fast? Or known where she was?

The liquid was upon her now, traveling up her body. She pushed at it, to no avail. It was thick, and the few portions she sloughed off were quickly replaced. She tried to block all her openings, but the liquid kept flowing, into her facial orifices, and others. She could feel it inside her, moving about, like a warm drink flowing down to her stomach, only terrible.

God, this was it. She could feel a pressure against her sinuses, her throat, her nasal cavities, everywhere. A stretching, as the liquid pushed against her. She'd be a red mist within seconds. Had the email gotten through?

Images flooded her mind. She stopped struggling. Then she was inside Terry, looking out somehow. Seeing Ray, and herself. Felt Terry communicating with Ray, days passing in a blur. Feeling its feelings. It all seemed so alien, yet paradoxically familiar somehow. She/it felt shame, and utter, utter sorrow. And then, a change. From almost suicidal wallowing to....just depressed, then okay, then even happy. Ray changed, too. At first he was frightening, monstrous. Then just slightly threatening, then likable, friendly. Then irritating, then piteous, and then, finally, contemptible. Her/its mood darkened. To annoyance and pique, then anger. Then this suppurated into violent fury. Other images appeared. More squonks, approaching, communicating. Then Terry, and the others budding, giving birth to young squonks, which grew impossibly fast. Then they in turn reproduced, on and on. She/it felt hoards of them, always multiplying. Then she/it were moving, mostly in liquid form. Attacking everything in their path. Insects, small animals, even bears were steadily engulfed, and then exploded from the inside. Then people. Ray, then strangers—men, women, and children. Even babies. Blood and body parts everywhere. Then a change. The squonks/her pulled back. They bulged within the people only enough to burst selected arteries and veins. Killing still, but more subtilely. Then the liquid mostly avoided bodily invasion, shorting out electrical systems, causing fires, or extinguishing pilot lights and causing death by gas inhalation, or gas explosions. Or hearts were squeezed, enough to kill, but not torn apart. Countless people were drowned by squonks in liquid form, while taking baths or swimming. People noticed, of course, and tried to hide in vehicles or buildings. Nothing worked. What structure is completely airtight? She/it witnessed numerous acts of futile bravery. People discharged guns, stabbed out with blades, all to no avail. How could they stop something that could dissolve, and then reform, whole again, at will, repeatedly? Some episodes were even tragicomic. A teen soaked up a liquid squonk in a huge sponge. A middle aged woman confused another by sucking it up in a Wet-Vac. These victories were short-lived, though, as the caged squonks simply reformed and burst out of their prisons. And more moving, traveling really. She/it invaded a sleeping man, yet stayed still, waiting, until he completed a plane ride, before emerging. More images of various rivers, coated with tiny grayish black slicks, which rode for a while, they moved over to beaches and docks, and then more victims. And all the while more and more, piling up, then moving out, flowing out in all directions. The emotions came into focus again. Complete, total hatred. Arrogant fury. Sadistic glee. The most savage of cruelties. Mocking her.

Simone fought, in her mind. Tried to push out thoughts, questions. Pleas, threats, anything. Nothing worked. She was overwhelmed almost before she started. She/they saw an image of herself, from outside again. Only now she was an obscenity, something pathetic, worthless. She was swept up in it, hating herself, disgusted by her very existence. She deserved no mercy, no sympathy, just hate, hate, hate.

It stopped. Her mind cleared. She could think her

own thoughts again. She looked around the apartment. It was filled with squonks. Dozens, maybe a hundred were perched everywhere. All facing her, with their grotesque, baggy and blemished bodies and nearly indistinguishable heads. This was it, she knew. Had the news gotten out, from her, or from the increasing amount of victims? Would people find a way to……

A huge cracking sound boomed. The walls, the furniture, everything in the room was covered in red spray and minuscule iotas of flesh. Three solid squonks now sat where Simone's body had been. They, and the rest of the blood spattered squonks all liquefied. Streams of grayish black liquid coursed through the apartment, seeking exit through the window cracks, or underneath the door. After only about a minute only red liquid remained.

The only sound was the ticking of the clock, and the steady dripping of blood off the ceiling and walls.

An Unusual Pet

Matt Hayward

"You're describing a triceratops."

The old man scratched at a dry patch on his forehead and leaned against the door. He clicked his tongue. "Sure, if that's what it sounds like to you. I'm just tellin' ya about Gordon."

Sarah laughed. "You call it *Gordon*, are you serious?"

Stepping onto the porch, he motioned to the open door. "Look, are you coming in or not? I've got work to do and I'm sure you don't have all day, neither."

"Of course, I'm sorry."

Sarah followed the man inside, the smell of grease and stale air attacking her senses. Black and white photos, sepia-toned with age, lined the walls. Class photos from the fifties froze smiling students in lined rows. Stacks of broken bicycles parts lay heaped beneath a staircase to the left like metal spaghetti.

"What did you say your name was again?" The old man asked, leading the way to a door on the far end of the hall.

"I didn't," Sarah said. "It's Sarah. Sarah Burke."

"And you're with your school newspaper or something?"

Her eyebrow arched in response. "No, I'm with *The Dublin Times*. Just started, actually. I used to be with a local paper."

"So you're from Ballydubh, originally?"

"Next town over, but Ballydubh was the nearest place with a newspaper so I started out here."

The old man entered the kitchen and presented the room with a flap of his arm. "Not much here, but it's enough. You like the Jesus painting there? Danny Porter did that for me."

Sarah couldn't help but chuckle. The painting depicted Jesus Christ with two muscular folded arms and the text DON'T CROSS ME scrolled beneath. She looked about the rest of the room, trying to hide her discomfort. A dozen fly-catching strips seeped from the ceiling, each caked in little black dots. More littered the floor. A dirty metallic dog bowl sat by the foot of the breakfast table, emptied of its contents.

"That's Gordon's, I'm guessing?"

The old man smiled. "Yup. Gordy loves the Pedigree with chicken bits. Ever try it yourself?"

"Dog food?"

"Ah, come on. I think everyone's wondered, no? I used to

try the new ones every time I got it for Gordon. Some of them weren't half bad."

Sarah folded her arms and eyed the old man. "Okay, now you're having me on. First, you describe a *triceratops*, for god's sake, and now tell me you're a connoisseur of canine grub."

The old man lowered to a seat by the table and sighed. He rubbed his hands together, making a sound like dry paper. "Why did you come here? Sit."

Sarah took the only other chair, a rickety looking thing, and removed her notepad and pen from her jacket pocket. "Rumors spread fast around this place, I'm sure you know. I still have a few friends in town and they told me you came across an *odd* pet. That's all they'd say. *Unusual.* Being where we are, I assumed it might be a deformed pig or some kind of farm animal, and I thought..." Sarah took a moment. "Well, I only started with *The Times*, okay? So, if I could raise awareness of an animal with a birth defect, maybe some folks would want to make donations and the public could pay for a life-changing operation. And if it wasn't a deformed pig or something, then... Well then I'd have a mighty good story, y'know?"

The old man lowed his eyes to slits, gauging her. "Why would you want to tell everyone about my Gordon, anyway?

Even if he is a *tri-top* or whatever you call it?"

"A *triceratops*! A dinosaur!"

"That what it is? So why would you want to tell everyone?"

Sarah removed her smart-phone and placed it on the center of the table. "You don't mind if I record this conversation, do you?"

The old man nodded to the phone. "What's that?"

"My smart-phone."

"Jaysus. That's not a phone. It's only the size of me palm."

Sarah's response fell away like a missed pinball.

"If it were a phone, then how would you be *recording sound*? That's a dicta-thing, or whatever you call it, that does that. Where do you plug it in?"

"It has a battery. Lasts long. There's an app that allows me to record conversations, just like a Dictaphone."

"So it's actually a dicta-*phone*?" The old man asked, nodding to Sarah while a smile spread across his weathered face.

"Jaysus..." Sarah rubbed at her forehead, the joke setting in. "It's got a camera, too," she added.

The old man brought his hands down on the table hard enough to make Sarah jump. He laughed, a noise not unlike a donkey. "A feckin' camera, in that thing? Now you're the one jokin' with me. What else does it do? Become a TV, as well?"

"Actually, yes... I suppose."

The old man's eyes widened. "Holy Mary... See, here you are, completely amazed that I might have a pet *three-tip* thing, and you're walking around with a Dictaphone, television and camera in your phone that's the size of a chocolate bar. And let me ask you again, why do you want to tell so many people about Gordon?"

Gordon. The name still made Sarah shake her head. "If you've *honestly* got a living triceratops in your backyard, the world's going to want to know. They've got a right to know."

"Why?" The old man asked. "What will they do if my Gordon is some old dinosaur or something? They'll come and take him away, won't they? And then what? Perform some mad tests or something. I won't even be allowed to visit."

This is insane, Sarah thought. *He's probably got a Rottweiler with pencils taped to its head out there...*

"It would be a marvel of the modern scientific world," she stated.

The old man snorted. "He'd be a freak. That's what'd happen."

"But you don't mind telling locals about him? If you *really* had a triceratops, you'd either run straight to a museum or keep it a secret. You wouldn't keep it like a dog."

"And why not? I told Danny and James and a few others in town, they all know. Told them because they're me mates. What are they going to do?"

"How can you be sure that these so-called *mates* wouldn't go and report it?"

"To who? Danny, I said. And James. *My friends.* Why would they go and do a thing like that? If you don't trust *your* mates, then you've got bad friends."

Good point, she thought.

"And they know it's here?"

"Sure. James brings back scraps from the butcher's every other Sunday for him. Loves the scraps, he does."

How? Sarah wondered. *How could it be possible for so many people to know of a living* triceratops *and not make international news? How?*

She answered her own question: *Because we're in the middle of nowhere in Ireland and these folks don't care about the outside world. They're quite content in their own little bubble. This is crazy...*

Still, she found herself asking the all-important question. "Can I see him?"

"Of course. I wouldn't let you go without seeing him if it's that important to ya. Come on. Mind the bits around the floor, I have them where I need them."

Sarah eyed the sideways spray cans and rolls of tape littering the linoleum as she followed the old man to the back door in the kitchenette. As he unbolted the door, his hands shaky, she asked, "What is it you do here, exactly?"

"Spray cars and bikes. Fix bicycles on the side, too. Danny drives down the vehicles he's repaired, and if they're in need of a paint touch up, I do it here in the backyard. Bought the house back in the Celtic boom so I don't have much bills. The work keeps me ticking over and busy. Just about. Although Gordon likes to annoy the shite out of me when I'm trying to get it done. Loves the roar of the engines, he does. There we go."

The old man nudged the door with his shoulder, cracking it open and allowing a fresh breeze inside. "Get's stuck on the floor mold sometimes when the weather changes. Wood expands. Come on out."

Sarah stepped into the back garden -- an acre of dead grass that led to the foot of the woodland in the distance. A worn

Toyota sat out in the open like an animal carcass, the driver door glistening in a fresh coat of black paint and lacquer. The old man's nearest neighbor appeared to be about a mile to the left.

"That's Danny's place," he said, noticing Sarah staring. "Garage is out back. He only has to bring the cars down that little stretch of road for me."

"And the woods? You ever go out there?"

The old man placed his hands on his hips and chuckled. "Every day. I've explored every square foot of that place throughout the years. It's where I found Gordon."

Sarah looked about the yard, trying to spot the creature. "Where is he now?"

Despite not trusting the old man's tale, a quiver of excitement still tickled her belly.

"It's his nap time. I'd say he's asleep in his house. I'll wake him in a sec."

"His *house?*"

"Sure. Looks like a doghouse. It's around the side there. James and Danny helped me slap it together last summer when I found him."

"And where *did* you find him?"

"Out there in the woods one day." The old man took a

seat on the porch, squinting out at the tree line. He removed a package of cigarettes from his jeans pocket and offered the box to Sarah. "Smoke?"

"Sure."

She took a cigarette and accepted the lighter, and once they both had their cigarettes lit, the old man continued.

"I was out there at about seven in the evening," he said, blowing smoke from his nostrils. "Trying to squeeze in a walk before dinner. There's an old creek that runs through, 'bout two miles in. Wanted to see it before heading home. Love the hidden rivers like that. Calm me, they do. So I'm walking through, and I start to hear these footsteps. *Clomp, clomp, clomp*, twigs snappin', leaves crunchin'. I'm not scared out there or anything, but I held me breath, stood still, thinkin' it might just be someone from town out for a walk, too. Then this *thing* just comes out of nowhere, starts coming towards me, about the size of a dog."

"Gordon?"

A broad smile lifted the man's weathered cheeks. "The little man hisself, lettin' out this squeaky wail of a sound. Falling forward on account of a gammy leg."

Sarah blew smoke. "*Gammy?*"

"Busted up," he explained. "Think he'd taken a fall

or something. I clicked me tongue, like how you'd call a dog, y'know?" He demonstrated, then added, "And he plodded on over. Went right past me and drank from the creek. Didn't seem to mind me at all. I bent down and stroked his head with my finger, like this." He waggled his index finger in the air. "He stopped drinkin' for a sec, but then went on. While he got some water in him, I went over and pulled a wad of grass, came back, and he took it from my hand. Jesus, my heart nearly exploded. Thing was feckin' adorable. Wait 'till you see."

Sarah couldn't keep the smile from her face. The old man's story played clear as a movie in her mind. Even if he *was* lying, she found him amusing and no longer cared if *Gordon* existed or not. She could always find another item for the paper, after all. A fluff piece. At least she spent an entertaining Saturday afternoon with an amusing individual.

"And how long have you had him now?" She asked, a laugh in her gut.

"Going on nearly a year. He's gotten a little bigger. Not much, mind, but a little. He's only 'bout the size of a regular dog. Not a little *ankle-biter*, as I call 'em, I mean a *real* dog. Like a Lab or something. 'Bout to my knee, there."

A noise from around the corner of the house caused

Sarah's chest to lurch. She planted her hands on the porch and got ready to stand.

The old man smiled. "There he is now. Think we must've woke him."

Sarah rose, her body tensing. Her mouth dried up. "He's not going to attack me, is he?" She asked. "Is he dangerous?"

The old man honked a laugh. "Jaysus, no! Sit down, ye mad thing. He's nice. Don't worry. That thing around his head, this, like, hard halo of a yolk, keeps banging off his door, that's all. Don't worry. Jaysus, you're jumpy as a tick."

Sarah spoke fast, her heart racing. "Tend to get that way around prehistoric creatures, yeah. Look, maybe I should go back inside and look out the window, see him from there?"

The old man flicked his finished cigarette butt into the yard and slowly got to his feet. "Ah would ye stop," he said. "Honestly, Gordon's grand. Look, here he is."

Sarah thought she'd pass out. She couldn't believe her eyes. Slinking towards them with a casual stride was a creature unlike anything she'd ever seen before. Except for illustrations. About the size of a dog, and with the skin of a lizard, Gordon yawned, its beak-like mouth quivering. Three tiny nubs jutted from its head, small, but with time, Sarah knew they'd eventually become horns. Horns sharp enough to pierce metal.

Sarah stared at the triceratops. And then her legs gave out.

She crashed to her rump on the porch and brought a shaking hand to her chest, trying to calm her erratic pulse. The dinosaur regarded her with sleepy glistening eyes, shook its head, then jogged forward. The jog became a trot, and the trot became a charge, head lowered.

"Gord!" The old man yelled. "None of that now!"

The dinosaur slowed, looking to them both frantically before raising to its hind legs and crashing back down. A low, mewling noise came from its mouth as a slim tongue slinked forth and licked its beak.

"He's just excited," the old man explained. "Happens when he meets someone new. He's getting better, though. Usually he'd piss all over the place. At least he's stopped that. Gordon, sit."

The dinosaur sat.

"This is insane," Sarah repeated before pushing herself from the porch. She crossed the yard cautiously, eyeing the creature with disbelief. "You've actually *domesticated* him." Glancing back at the old man, she asked, "Is it okay to pet him?"

"Of course." He rose with a grunt and crossed to her side. "Give him a good rub on the ol' head. Loves that."

Sarah got to one knee. The triceratops stared her in the eye but stayed put, barely. It squirmed as if full of electricity. She reached out with one hand and gingerly stroked the creature's head, the scaly skin bumpy beneath her fingers. "He likes it? This is amazing."

"It's just my Gordon. Loves the greens, too. Want to feed him a lettuce head?"

"Sure," Sarah said. She got to her feet. "Aren't triceratops herbivores?"

"Huh?"

"I mean, don't they eat only vegetables?"

The old man scratched his chin and squinted. "Say, maybe that's why he's been having stomach problems lately. The damn dog food... Gees, I'm sorry, lad. From now on I'll stick to the greens. Thanks, love. I'll be back in a moment."

"Sure..."

The old man returned to the house and rummaged about in the fridge. Sarah listened to him whistle. She stayed put and kept eye contact with the creature, still feeling as if in a dream. The possibility of exposing this discovery to the world refused to leave her mind. She thought of the seconds she had alone, looked back to the creature -- and then eased her phone from her jeans. She gave a quick glance back towards the house before opening her camera app and snapping a couple of photos. Her hands shook too much at first, but with a breath, she got a clear and focused image. The dinosaur sat still, watching the object in her hand with something close to amusement. Satisfied with the final picture, she slipped the phone back into her pocket and clasped her hands behind her back.

"Here," the old man said, returning with a head of lettuce. "I'll let you do it."

Sarah took the vegetable and kept her expression neutral, hoping the old man didn't notice the sweat now beading from her pores. She then fed the creature, watching in amazement as it finished the snack within a few short mouthfuls. Finished, it squawked.

"No more now," the old man warned with a pointed finger. "Gotta keep from overfeeding you. Else you get as fat as a couch one day."

Sarah turned to him. "You know he's going to get bigger and bigger, right? Larger than a couch."

"Larger than a couch, you say?"

"You haven't thought about that? What the future will hold?"

The old man shook his head. "I just live in the moment. Don't see no point in worrying about the future. It might hold all sorts, but that doesn't concern me. I'm happy tinkering about here with Gord and the cars."

Sarah didn't have a response.

"Besides," the old man continued. "Dicta-phones and cameras and TVs all in one, all that email stuff, the internet in general... Just makes my head spin. Hell, I'm happy with my VHS player for movies. I think all the best ones have been made, anyway. Haven't seen a good picture made past the seventies." He looked at Sarah closely. "Speaking of which, I wanted to get this car finished up and sent back to Danny so I can catch the end of a film. Is there anything else you wanted?"

Sarah shook her head. "No, I guess not... Thanks for having me over. And for introducing me to Gordon."

The old man smiled. "Our pleasure. Honestly. If you want to stop by and see him again, get in touch."

"I will."

"Can I ask you something?"

Sarah was caught off guard by the question. "Sure?" She

said.

"After all you've told me, now I'm getting worried you'll do a write up about my Gordon and folks will come by to see him... Folks I don't want to see him. Never thought about it much, but after all you've said, I'm worried they'll take him away. Please keep Gordon to yourself."

Sarah looked to the creature and back to the old man. "I will. You've got nothing to worry about."

"Thank you. Come back sometime soon, yeah? We can take him for a walk."

"I'd like that."

Sarah made her way back to the front of the house, the sound of the old man chatting to his pet fading in the distance. She slipped her key from her pocket and pressed the fob, unlocking her car. Once she climbed in and closed her door, she sighed.

Looking out the windshield, she eyed the old man's house. An unkempt bungalow like so many others she'd passed on the drive from Dublin -- the kind of place she'd not give a second glance on an average day. She'd never have guessed that, out back, lived a creature capable of changing mankind's understanding of the world.

252

Grinning, she fished her phone from her pocket and opened the photo she'd snapped. The picture came out perfect, a high-resolution of Gordon sitting on the dead grass, his eyes trained on the camera. Her stomach fluttered as the image of revealing her discovery to her editor swam to the surface of her mind. She imaged the disappointment in the old man's face. Imagined Gordon stressed as he was subjected to needles and prodding and flashing cameras.

Cameras.

She thought of the device in her hands, another marvel of the world folks took for granted on a daily basis. Then the old man's *dicta-phone* joke made her smile.

The photos were undeniable, to show them to an expert would lead to an investigation, no doubt. And within a day, those same experts would bore down on the old man's house. Changing everything. They'd take Gordon away.

Her finger hovered above the delete button.

"We've got enough we don't appreciate," she muttered. "No use digging up the past."

Sarah took one final, close look at the picture before jabbing *delete*. Her stomach gave a lurch, her mind reeling with the possibility of having made a mistake.

Then the phone prompted, *are you sure?*

Sarah laughed. "Yes," she answered. "I'm sure."

She deleted the photo, put the car in gear, and reversed from the driveway, leaving the ancient past where it belonged.

Finding a Purpose

Jaleta Clegg

"You're fired! Fired, fired, fired!" Flecks of spittle dotted Mr. Laredo's receding chin. "Two weeks you've worked for me and I've lost more business than in the ten years previously. Fired!" He stabbed the air with his finger.

"I am sorry, Mr. Laredo." Arnold's ponderous voice filled the room.

Mr. Laredo's secretary shivered as she slid the pink slip onto Arnold's desk. She retreated to her own corner, shooting glances at the large, lumpy man in the battered trench coat and stained fedora.

"I truly did not mean to lose your business. I am certain I can find it again." Arnold hunched in his trench coat, shame lowering his head.

"Get out!" Mr. Laredo pointed to the door.

Arnold rose, looming over Mr. Laredo though he tried not to. His claws fumbled across the desk before he managed to grip the pink slip and tuck it into the trench coat's pocket. He shuffled under the sign proclaiming Laredo Life Insurance Agency, the Best in the West, into the dusty street beyond. He pulled his fedora lower over his bare skull.

The sleepy desert town drowsed in the summer heat. Clouds built over the far range of mountains that ringed the dry valley, puffy white but with a darker, more sinister shading to their bellies. Arnold shuffled down the street, his claws clicking on the cement sidewalk.

"I have no purpose," he told the dog growling behind a white picket fence. The dog tucked his tail between his legs and retreated as far as his chain would allow. Arnold shoved his claws into his pockets. Children and animals saw his true form. Adults saw what they wanted to see, unable to believe the truth. Children and animals ran in fear from his presence. Adults reacted with shouting, usually.

The Burger Bonanza sported a 'help wanted' sign. Arnold paused, but only for a moment. He'd worked for one day at a chicken restaurant in a town farther north. After he pulled chicken from the deep fryer with his bony claws that passed for hands, the other worker fainted. The owner called the police. Arnold fled, hitchhiking his way to a new town and new opportunities. No, Burger Bonanza would not be a suitable place to find his purpose. Selling Mr. Laredo's life insurance policies had not been his purpose, either.

Arnold shuffled his way through the town, up the hill to the old graveyard. Death was comfortable, and comforting. He dusted off an old marker. "Henry Cluff will not mind if I rest here while I ponder my purpose for existence."

Arnold hunched on the gravestone, a shapeless figure in an oversized trench coat and smashed fedora. The wind teased the tails of his coat and the untrimmed grass of the neglected cemetery. The town sprawled below, a grid of streets where little moved in the heat of the afternoon. A truck crawled along the freeway on the far side, heat waves distorting the view. Thunderclouds built over the far range of mountains.

A ground squirrel darted over a toppled stone, pausing near the grave, tiny paws tucked across its chest. It cocked its head, as if listening.

Arnold took this as a positive sign. "I need a purpose. My creator died before he could give me my purpose. I am not suited to selling life insurance or cooking chicken. Or selling mattresses or arranging flowers or even delivering pizza."

The squirrel froze, eyes wide in terror. It squeaked an alarm, dashing into the bushes.

Arnold sighed, a gust tasting of old death.

Lightning flashed in the clouds. Delayed thunder rumbled, low and threatening. The rising wind tugged his fedora from his head, tumbling it along the ground. Arnold turned his head to watch. His naked skull gleamed. He flexed his claws, digging grooves in the overgrown grass.

"I should retrieve my hat, but somehow, I do not feel any compulsion to do so. I feel adrift."

The weeds gave no response.

Lightning erupted from the dark thunderheads. Thunder boomed. A fireball spat from the cloud, arcing towards Arnold. He watched it streak closer, flames burning through the sky.

"Perhaps I am to die in fire."

The fireball roared, resolving into a winged Harley. A buxom blonde in a horned helmet clutched the handlebars, her face frozen in a scream of rage.

Arnold cocked his skull. He'd never been good at thinking. It took much effort. Perhaps because his creator had not gifted him with a brain, only reflexes. "I wish I knew why I was made," he told the flaming apparition as it approached.

The motorcycle slammed into the old cemetery, plowing a furrow through the gravestones, the frame crumpling. The blonde woman rolled free, tumbling across the graveyard in a sprawl of shapely limbs. She bounced to her feet, stamping and shouting ancient Nordic curses at the clouds. Her long braids swung as she shook her fist at the thunderclouds. She wore a very short skirt and a breastplate. No, Arnold corrected himself, breast bowls. They were much too rounded and curvy to be called plates.

The woman noticed him and paused, lowering her fist. She brushed a stray strand of hair from her cheek. "What the hell are you?"

"I am Arnold." Arnold lifted the broken horn of her helmet from the weeds with one delicate claw. He offered it to the woman.

She narrowed her eyes, ignoring the horn. "You stink of death."

"It is to be expected. I am a tupilak." She saw him for what he truly was. Perhaps she also knew the reason he was created. He felt a twinge of excitement at the thought. His heart would have raced, if he'd had one.

"What in the fimble winter is a tupilak?"

"I am. My creator assembled me from the bones and skins of animals. I have the agility of a hare, the cunning of a fox, the strength of a bear, the speed of a falcon, the stealth of an owl, the stamina of a caribou, and the vision of an eagle." Arnold tipped his head in a polite nod. "My name is Arnold."

She pulled the battered helmet from her head, scratching a hand over her scalp. "No wonder you smell of death."

"My creator died after giving me spirit but before giving me purpose. Do you perhaps know my purpose?" Arnold's empty eye sockets searched her face.

"Don't know and don't care." She jammed her helmet back on her head. "I've got work to do."

"Perhaps I could assist you in your work?"

She tugged her short leather skirt into place. "What do you know about gathering souls?"

Arnold shrugged. "I know how to deep fry chicken and how to fill out claim forms. I tried to sell brooms once. I do not know about souls." A tickle of buried instinct stirred inside his empty skull. "It sounds somewhat familiar, though."

Thunder boomed overhead. Lightning stabbed the ground.

The woman shouted curses to the storm. "I'm supposed to collect the soul of Bud Gruber the plumber to take to Valhalla. The pipes are so backed up not even Thor can knock the crap loose. A thousand years of paradise and partying leaves its mark. My name's Hildebørg, by the way."

"It is a pleasure to make your acquaintance, Hildebørg." Arnold tripped over the odd name, his semi-mummified tongue unable to twist around the correct pronunciation. "How do you collect souls?"

"I wait until they are about to die, then offer them an invitation. An eternity of partying with beautiful young Valkyries, all the feasting you can handle, plus you get to hear Odin's jokes. I don't tell them how bad those are. Or how outdated the plumbing is at Valhalla, among other things."

Lightning stabbed the gate of the cemetery. Sparks flew. Hildebørg's hair crackled, standing on end.

"Thrice cursed Thunder sisters, you can't have him! Bud Gruber is mine, dammitall!" Hildebørg kicked at the smoldering weeds. "You totaled my bike, you bitches!" She shouted more curses at the storm, shaking her fist violently over her head.

Arnold wondered at the valkyrie's passionate swearing. He'd never heard the like. Not even Mr. Laredo could swear that impressively. "What is stopping you from collecting his soul?"

"They are!" She stabbed her finger at the roiling thunderhead.

Arnold applied his eagle vision. Two women, dressed only in the billowing clouds, lounged in the gray mass. Black hair swirled on the vicious winds. Their laughter echoed in the thunder. Arnold wished he had been gifted with the knowledge of a sage. He tilted his head, comparing the cloud women to Hildebørg. They seemed large and shapeless, next to her hard muscle and shapely breast bowls. He pondered the distinction. "You appear stronger."

"They've got control of air and fire. I've got the ability to pull a soul from a dying body. No comparison. I've run afoul of them before. Sadistic bitches. I tried to talk Thor into loaning me his hammer. It wasn't like I asked him to hand over his balls. Stupid man. My weapons won't touch them. I was hoping to sneak in while they were occupied with starting a forest fire."

Arnold flexed his bony claws. "Do you wish them to die? I know a great deal about death."

"Considering you're made of death, I don't doubt you. But the Thunder Sisters are immortal. They can't die, but they can feel pain. I got my hands on a really sweet flamethrower a few months back. Worked on the air sister. Maybe if I got a big tank of liquid nitrogen, I could freeze them both." She watched Arnold's wicked claws. "They're tied to the Southwest US so I don't have to deal with them very often. But you, I've never run into your kind before. How do the rules apply to you?"

"I do not know. I was not given much knowledge. I have tried to learn, but without a brain, I cannot hold much. Mr. Laredo fired me because I could not sell life insurance."

"You tried to sell life insurance?" Hildebørg grinned.

"I was not successful. Too many clients smelled death in my presence, though they did not recognize it. Humans see only what they expect to see, not what is truly before them. Except for the children. They see the truth."

A blast of wind surged through the cemetery, whipping the smoldering weeds into open flame.

"That tears it. Those bitches are going to get exactly what they deserve." Hildebørg clenched both fists. "Except I've got no way to get to them. They blasted my Harley. It was a special edition, the Valhalla Touring Cycle. They don't make those anymore. I don't know how I'm getting back now." She kicked the prone motorcycle. Chrome flashed, reflecting a streak of lightning.

Arnold tapped his claw on the gravestone. Heat from flames and summer washed over his bones. "I desire a purpose. You desire the end of the Thunder Sisters. Give me a purpose,

Hildebørg of the Valkyries."

Lightning stabbed the hill around the cemetery. Flames roared in the overgrowth of bushes and dry grass. Wind whipped the Valkyrie's hair. The Thunder Sisters' laughter mocked them both.

Hildebørg planted her hands on her hips. "Arnold Tupilak, I wish the destruction of the Thunder Sisters, or at least a good trouncing. Is that enough of a purpose?"

"Revenge for the destruction of your motorcycle?" Red fire blossomed in his empty eye sockets.

"And for getting in my way once too often."

Arnold snarled, springing from the confines of his trench coat His eye sockets burned with red light. He flexed his wicked claws. Death flowed from him, quenching the fires, driving back the wind and the lightning. He sprang, leaping into the air towards the clouds.

Hildebørg watched him rise, mouth hanging open in awe. "I'll be damned."

The Thunder Sisters saw the apparition that was Arnold, burning with red light that dripped like blood from his bare bones and shreds of rotting skin and feathers. They tried to retreat but their own storm trapped them over the valley. Arnold tore into them, claws shredding their substance to tatters. Their screams echoed like the shrieks of damned souls.

Hildebørg crouched, clapping hands over her ears.

The thundercloud boiled as the Thunder Sisters fought back. Tornado fingers reached from the cloud, stubby and unable to reach the ground. The air reeked of ozone. Lightning crackled through the cloud. The sky dimmed to a sickly greenish purple.

Arnold swooped through the cloud, blazing with red fire. He sucked a tornado into his skull, shooting it out at the sisters. The sisters sent sheets of fire and air battering his skeleton. Shreds of old skins ripped free, raining across the town in smoldering tufts. Arnold spread wings made from dead owls, returning the attack. The air sister erupted in flames, tall and white as wild lightning. She shrieked, crumpling and fading like a spent thundercloud.

The fire sister wailed. Jagged bolts of fire walked the hills, falling from the cloud like Zeus' legendary bolts. Hildebørg ducked behind the biggest tombstone, shield clutched tightly in one hand.

Arnold the tupilak drew in more tornado vortices, pulling lightning to dance inside his empty ribcage. He spread his tattered wings, flaps of dead skin waving in the fierce air currents.

He opened his mouth.

The fire sister rammed a gigantic fist into his open jaw.

Arnold's fire dimmed as his attack backfired, blasting him from the inside. He tumbled from the cloud, a battered skeleton pieced from bits of death.

Hildebørg saw her chance dying with Arnold the tupilak. "Arnold! Cunning of a fox, strength of a bear, stamina of a caribou, whatever the hell that is—you can beat them!"

Arnold's wings snapped open. His eye sockets blazed red. He darted to the cloud, banking away at the last second. The sisters screamed in rage. Wind blasted the valley. Arnold circled high, climbing to the top of the thunderhead. The sisters rose in pursuit. Arnold folded his wings, diving into the center of the cloud, red fire trailing. The cloud boiled, red and black. Wind roared through the sky. Lightning danced in wild displays. Arnold disappeared into the roiling mass.

Air, Fire, and Death collided, tearing each other to shreds in a display of raw power. Hildebørg cowered by the gravestone as thunder split the sky. The backlash of the explosion slammed her to the ground.

As quickly as the storm had broken, it subsided. The wind stilled. The cloud melted to nothing. Wisps of smoke rose from the blackened grasses. Hildebørg raised her head. A fine sifting of ash drifted on the summer afternoon. A single siren wailed in the town. She rose to her feet, brushing dirt from her leather skirt. The tupilak couldn't possibly have survived the explosion, but he'd at least cleared the way for her to gather the soul of Bud Gruber the plumber. The Thunder Sisters wouldn't be bothering anyone for quite some time.

"Hildebørg, have I done well?"

She spun around.

Arnold posed on the gravestone, a satisfied curl to his bony jaw. "Have I served my purpose?"

"In spades." Hildebørg brushed stray grass from her curvaceous breast bowls.

Arnold cocked his head. "Why am I not disintegrating? Once a tupilak has fulfilled its purpose, it should dissipate. I should no longer be animate."

"Do you want another purpose?" Hildebørg adjusted her breast bowls. "I've got more souls to collect and the competition can be fierce. I'd love to have you on my side."

"You are offering me a job?"

"Definitely."

"We should discuss terms of employment. I wish at least

one week a year of vacation."

The Valkyrie frowned. "What would you do with vacation time?"

"I do not know, but it is standard and acceptable practice. You will need to write a contract that I may sign. I learned that from Mr. Laredo. Always get it in writing."

"You should argue politics with Loki. I think he'd lose for once." She pulled his trench coat from a bush, flipping it to him. "I hope Bud is still around. Plumbers are difficult to find."

"Plumbers are always late. Mr. Laredo complained many times about plumbers. And lawyers. Do we need to collect one of those?" Arnold slipped the trench coat over his bones.

"Odin All-Father would string me up naked and throw stones at me if I brought a lawyer to Valhalla." Hildebørg grunted as she pulled her Harley upright. One wing hung crooked, broken spokes protruding. "Dammitall, now I have to find a mechanic. Think Bud Gruber would mind waiting?"

"I am certain if you promise him eternal parties and beautiful women he would not mind waiting." Arnold placed his battered fedora on his naked skull.

"Hang on a sec." Hildebørg pulled a small device from a pocket in her skirt. She tapped the screen. "Bud Gruber is going to have company. His best friend, Larry Hubert, is a mechanic. Both are scheduled to perish in a house fire."

Sirens wailed through the town. Smoke rose in a dark plume.

Hildebørg frowned. "We're not supposed to interfere like that. Bud was supposed to choke on his french fries, not perish in a fire."

Arnold shrugged. "It was not your fault. It was the Thunder Sisters. They started the fires. Is there a punishment? I do not know the rules."

Hildebørg put her device back into her pocket. She pushed her Harley through the weeds to the cemetery gate. "Don't worry about it. I'll tell you if you need to know." The bike snagged on a buried stone. The valkyrie swore as she tried to tug it free.

Arnold placed a delicate claw on the seat, only tearing it a little as he pushed the motorcycle free. "You do not follow rules much, do you?"

"Only when it suits me. And when I won't get caught." Hildebørg grinned. "You're going to like Valhalla."

"Perhaps I could learn plumbing."

They walked from the cemetery, the shapely Valkyrie and

the hunched tupilak, down a path of golden light cast by the setting sun.

Arnold's back was straighter, his bare skull held high. He had finally found his purpose.

Devils in the Dark

JG Faherty

No matter how hard Eddie Kemper scrubbed, the stench of the beast refused to go away, clinging to his hands like the memories lingered in his head.

The creature spotlighted in his high beams. Brakes squealing as he slammed his foot on the pedal. The acrid smell of burning rubber. The sickening thump of metal striking flesh.

The face... Part monkey, part dog...the long snout filled with dangerous-looking teeth. Pointed ears, like a Doberman's. Deadly claws as long as his fingers. And the eyes...

Even now, two hours later, the thought of those horrible orbs sent shivers through him. Black as night but somehow filled with intelligence and fury as the creature stared up at him, its legs twisted and broken, dark, foamy spit oozing from its mouth. Then the life had faded from them, leaving only a bloody corpse.

And the stink.

It was the worst thing he'd ever smelled, like being in a monkey house in the summer, only all the monkeys were dead and bloated. He'd had to stop and puke twice while lifting the body into his truck – no easy feat, considering it was as big as a damn German shepherd – and then drive with the windows open until he reached the motel.

Eddie rubbed the cheap soap over his flesh again, working up a heavy lather. Although he'd never graduated high school, he had enough smarts to recognize a potential windfall when it landed in his lap. And the dead thing in the back of his '69 El Camino might just be the answer to his dreams of getting filthy rich. He'd done plenty of hunting over the years, but he'd never seen nothin' like the thing he'd hit on Highway 77.

Which meant it could be valuable to the right people.

Which was why as soon as he picked up the two pounds of weed from his cousin Max in Bucksboro, he was heading straight to that big college in Charleston instead of back to North Carolina. There had to be some scientist folks who'd pay major cash for whatever the hell it was he'd found.

Eddie thrust his hands under the hot water.

Now if only he could get rid of the smell...

Max Wayne stared at the monster in the truck and gave a long whistle.

"Dude, when you said you had a problem, I didn't expect nuthin' like this."

You don't know the half of it, Eddie felt like telling his cousin. There'd been nothing but problems since he'd hit the damn thing. He'd arrived at Max's house only to find out from Mary-Ellen, Max's dim-witted nag of a wife, that Max was working a double at the Fayette County Fair, repairing generators and wiring the sound stage, and he had the weed with him. He'd driven to the carnival, where he'd had to wait two hours before Max took lunch, the whole time imagining the monkey-dog thing swelling up inside its tarp like a dead deer on the highway, getting ready to split open and spill its guts all over.

Then, on top of everything, Max had told him he didn't want to transfer the weed until it got dark, so they'd have to wait until he got off at midnight. Eddie knew the body wouldn't last that long, not with the temperature already creeping towards ninety. Which meant letting Max in on the secret. When he'd lifted the tarp up, the explosion of stink had made them both gag. After tying a handkerchief over his face, Max leaned in for a closer look.

"Damn, cuz...you know what you got there?"

"Nope. It jumped in front of me on the highway last night. Like a freakin' kangaroo. I never had a chance to stop."

"That there's a devil monkey, dude. Didn't think they was real." Max waved his hand and a cloud of flies rose up. "Sure does stink, don't it?"

"Devil monkey? You pullin' my leg?"

"That's what the old-timers call 'em. Every few years someone'll say they seen one. The paper runs a story about boogems and monsters in the woods and everyone has a good laugh. Now you gone and bagged one!"

"Well, I ain't heard of no devil monkey, but I know this thing ain't natural. I'm takin' it up to Charleston to see if one of the colleges will buy it."

"How much you think it's worth?"

Eddie heard the greed in his cousin's voice. There was no getting around splitting the profits, not if he wanted help.

Of course, Max didn't have to know what those profits were...

"A couple of hundred, I figure." Eddie figured it was worth at least three times that. "I gotta keep it fresh, though. I need ice. You help me, I'll give you half."

Max turned to him and smiled.

"Ice? I can do a whole lot better than that."

Eddie sipped his lemonade, relishing the way the sweet-and-sour liquid carved a cold, wet gully through the desert in his throat.

For once, Max had come through for him. The dead monkey-thing was wrapped up nice and tight in its tarp in the snack bar's walk-in freezer, hidden behind racks of frozen burgers, fries, and hot dogs. With the worry of decomposition gone, Eddie was able to relax and enjoy the day, mostly by eating junk and listening to the latest hits by Foreigner and Skynyrd and Queen and Aerosmith blasting out of the fairground speakers. Hearing "Dream On" played at near ear-splitting levels had helped him make another decision.

He was going to take some of the money he made from selling his devil monkey and buy a cassette deck and some kick-ass speakers for the El Camino.

No more eight-tracks for Eddie Kemper.

After downing the last of the lemonade, Eddie checked his watch. Almost five. The demolition derby didn't start 'til eight. After it was over, he and Max would load up the body and he could hit the road. He'd get the weed on the way back home.

As he walked across the fair grounds to the racetrack, he was already thinking about how to spend the rest of his money.

Behind the wooden platform that served as the concert stage, Max Wayne's walkie-talkie crackled to life.

"Max? We got another gennie that just blew. Where are you?"

Max let out a long, slow exhale, savoring the way the pot smoke burned his throat and tongue. Then he thumbed the talk button on the radio.

"Still at the stage. Ain't nearly done yet."

He'd actually finished checking the amps and lights a half hour ago, but what was the point of busting your butt on a wicked hot night? Let someone else worry about the damn generator. He was finishing his break.

He closed his eyes again and returned to his hazy daydreams of how much money he'd have after Eddie sold that freaky monkey.

It never occurred to him to ask which generator had

blown.

"Do you smell that?" Evan June sniffed the air, his face wrinkling from the foul odor attacking his nostrils.

"Something's dead," Grady Bach said.

"Yeah." Evan aimed his flashlight at the deep freeze, where one of the fry cooks was just coming out with a box of hamburgers. "I think it's coming from inside the freezer."

Grady shrugged. "Better take a look."

Evan nodded. Looking for a dead animal in a dark room on the hottest night of the summer wasn't high on his list of things he wanted to do. But it appeared they didn't have a choice, not unless they wanted to spend the next hour working in a room that stunk worse than road kill.

Stepping carefully because melting ice had made the metal floor slick as a December sidewalk, Evan worked his way through the freezer, flashlight moving back and forth, sniffing the air as he went.

"It's coming from back here," he said, stepping around a rack full of boxes. A sudden fear rose up in him, the product of too many scary movies where someone stumbled across a dead body.

"Holy Jesus," he whispered. Behind him, Grady echoed his words and added several others.

It was a body on the floor all right, but not human. Evan could tell that just from the two hairy feet sticking out of the rolled-up tarp.

"It smells like it's been dead for a month." Grady waved his hand in front of his face. "I hope that ain't what they're cooking."

"We gotta see what it is." Evan knelt down, using his free hand to tug open the tarp. After a moment, Grady joined him and they unwrapped the body.

"What in the hell...?" Evan's voice trailed off as he stared at the thing. His first thought was someone'd killed a monkey. But a closer look revealed it was no monkey they'd found. Not with those wicked claws and dog-like snout.

Evan reached out towards it.

"What are you doing?" Grady grabbed his wrist.

"I just wanna see if it's real. Maybe someone put it here as a joke." Evan poked it with a finger.

And screamed when its eyes opened.

The creature attacked so quickly Evan had no time

to react. He fell backwards, his second cry nothing but a wet choking sound as blood spurted from a jagged slit in his neck and painted the walls and floor.

Grady tried to crawl away but white-hot agony filled his left calf. He rolled over and saw chunks of his leg stuck to the creature's dagger-like claws.

Movement near the door caught his attention and he waved the flashlight at it.

"Help me," he called to the figure, which was only a shadow against the dark night sky. "Please!"

The figure moved closer, stepping into the dim glow of the light. Grady gasped.

It was a twin to the creature on the tarp.

And it wasn't alone.

"Hey, I wonder what all the commotion's about?"

Max motioned with his beer towards a spot in the center of the fairgrounds, where the telltale flashing lights of police cars outshone the neon of the rides and booths.

Eddie turned around. From their seats at the top of the bleachers, they had a perfect view of the fair and the racetrack.

He grimaced as he wiped grit from his eyes and caught a whiff of devil monkey. Even though he'd washed a dozen times after he and Max hid the body, the smell refused to go away.

"What's over there?" he asked.

"Yes!" Max pumped his fist as two cars collided in the center of the track. "I dunno. The arcade? Or maybe the snack bar."

A chill ran through Eddie. "The snack bar? You mean, where we hid...you know?"

"Relax, dude." Max chugged some beer. "No one's gonna find our payday. It's hidden behind, like, a thousand burgers."

"So why are the cops there?" Eddie couldn't keep his eyes off the swirling lights. The rumble of super-charged engines and the thundering crash of metal on metal faded into the background as he tried to see why people were running in all directions.

Then he saw them. Shadows leaping and darting among the crowds. Coming closer. Disappearing under the bleachers.

Someone screamed.

Another voice joined the first. Then others.

A second later, all hell broke loose.

"Watch out!" Max shouted, as someone ran into him,

knocking the beer from his hand in the process. The pounding of hundreds of feet on the metal bleachers drowned out the growls of sawed-off exhausts. All around them was total chaos, people running in all directions. Some fell and got trampled by the fleeing crowd. Others tumbled down rows of stairs, the sound of their breaking bones lost in the riotous din.

His eyes dull and wide from pot and confusion, Max turned his head back and forth, trying to make sense of what was happening.

Eddie didn't bother. He knew.

They were coming for him.

The relatives of the thing he'd killed. Somehow, its pack had found him, followed him all the way to Bucksboro.

He spotted them as they leapt onto the bleachers like pint-sized kangaroos, a dozen of them at least. Others hopped the barrier fence right into the racetrack. Cars swerved and slid on the hard-packed dirt, smashing each other worse than during the derby itself. That was when Max finally noticed them.

"Holy...Eddie, did you see that? It's..."

Max's voice faded away as he saw the ones climbing the bleachers. The combined reek of the animals hit Eddie like a punch in the stomach and he vomited up his hot dogs and beer.

Next to him, Max gagged and put his arm over his face.

From ten feet away, one of them stared straight at Eddie, its black eyes blazing with hatred. It took another step, and the pack behind it followed in unison.

"Screw this!" Max darted to the right, heading for the closest stairs. He made it only three steps before one of the devil monkeys bounded into the air and landed on his back. Max let out a strangled cry that came to an abrupt end when the creature tore his throat out.

Eddie took a step back and the pack moved another step forward. When Eddie tried to step away again, the back of his legs hit the low protective railing that marked the top of the bleachers.

The troop advanced another step.

"I didn't mean it!" Eddie shouted at them. "It was an accident. I'm sorry!"

The lead monkey leaned closer, its lips drawn back to expose over-large teeth. It raised its hands, displaying certain death. The others did the same.

Another step. It was close enough now to touch Eddie without extending its arm all the way. Eddie closed his eyes, not caring that he was crying, not caring that he'd wet his pants, his only thought that he didn't want to die like this.

The barnyard reek filled his nose and coated his tongue. Rough flesh, like the pads of a dog's foot, pressed against his arms and chest. He pictured them all around him, claws ready to tear him to pieces.

His body was in the air before he realized they'd pushed him over the railing. His body tumbled over and then a terrible agony exploded in his legs, accompanied by a crack like a tree splitting in a storm. He tried to scream but the pain stole the air from his lungs and all he could do was dig his fingers into the dirt and moan.

How long he lay there, he had no idea. A minute? Five? Time didn't exist, nothing existed, only the pain that grew worse each time he moved. It was the stink of the beasts that made him open his eyes. Their leader stood before him again. Only this time it held something in its arms.

The one he'd hit. Alive.

Even through the red haze of his agony, he recognized it. It glared with the same hatred as the others, its legs hanging broken and useless.

Eddie glanced at himself and saw white bone sticking out of pale flesh.

The pack turned as one and bounded away. In seconds, he was alone.

We're the same, he thought. For now. But not for long.

Because no animal could survive those kinds of injuries without medical care. Sooner or later, it would die. And when it did, they'd be back.

It was just a matter of time.

Spider

A. Collingwood

I met Jin on the night my first wife died; I just didn't realize it at the time. Karen, my first wife, was killed by a spider bite while we were on vacation in Japan. Waking up that night I had the greatest shock I had at up until that point in my life; the spider that killed her was sitting on her forehead, still as a stone, watching me sleep. It was big, brown, hairy, and it had eight green eyes which were staring right at me.

It is one of my biggest regrets that the big furry bastard got away before I could smash it.

I grabbed at the first thing I could find, a glass of water on the night table, and flung it at the spider, but all I did was succeed in splashing water across Karen's face. The little devil was gone.

"Sorry honey, there was a giant bug right on your head," I said quickly, before I could get an earful for waking her up like that. But she wasn't angry, she wasn't anything but cold.

I don't know why, but my first response was to call the

front desk. Kind of fucked up, isn't it? But I was worried that 911 wasn't the right number to call in Japan, so I called the front desk and made them call for me. Within minutes my room was swarming with first bellboys, then the hotel manager, then paramedics, then men in polyester jackets that put Karen into a bag and took her away.

I spent the next year of my life numb, as if the spider's venom had gotten into me too, and shut down all my emotions. Then, one day, sitting at my office at the bank, talking to a young man about what sort of financing options were available for starting a board game café, when it hit me. Karen was never going to play Scrabble again. She loved Scrabble. Like, she fucking loved Scrabble. She even had the Scrabble app on her phone. And she was never going to play Scrabble again. Never ever.

I was crying so hard that I didn't even notice the young man leaving, or my boss coming into the room, or him writing a note telling me to call him when I was ready and placing it by my hand.

When I did notice all these things I went to the washroom, washed my face, and went back to my desk to dial Greg's extension. I greeted him in a broken voice.

"Hey, George, how are you feeling, buddy?"

"I'm sorry, Greg, I don't know what happened there. I just... I don't know, it caught up with me. I can reschedule my appointments for-"

"Hey, whoa, slow down there big guy," Greg interrupted. "This sort of thing happens, you hear about it all the time. When Karen died you never really grieved, you just came back and started right back in. The truth is we've all been worried about you. So, tell you what, you were entitled to four weeks bereavement leave last year, as far as I'm... hang on a sec, I'm coming to your office."

Greg clicked the phone down, and I was left to sit awkwardly when he popped open my door, wearing a sympathetic frown. Greg was short, enthusiastic, and four years younger than me, the fucker. He came and sat himself on the edge of my desk.

"Hey buddy," he said sympathetically, "How are you feeling?"

"Fine, fine, look I really don't--"

"Let me stop you right there, George," interrupted Greg. "You were entitled to four weeks bereavement leave, and I really think you should take it now. I can pull some strings, no problem."

Greg gave me a serious, yet oddly smirking look.

"You have to take care of this," he said, tapping on his chest around the area of his heart. "Before you can take care of this."

He patted the desk meaningfully. Suddenly I couldn't stay in that office another day.

"You know what? That sounds great. I think that's just what I need."

"Great, do me a favor and switch over any appointments you have to Renee, then you go ahead and get out of here, alright buddy? We'll see you in April."

"Sure, yeah, thanks Greg."

When I got home that afternoon, I cracked open a beer, sat in my easy chair and turned on the TV like I have every day since Japan. I turned it off immediately.

Instead I left my beer sweating on the table and walked through the house. I hadn't done a thing with it since Karen died. I think six months ago I dusted, and once in a while I swept, but all the furniture was the same, all the pictures were still there, and all her clothes were right where I had left them.

I walked into the closet, thinking that her smell would surround me, that I would feel like she was all around me again. I closed my eyes and breathed in… nothing.

She wasn't there at all.

I tore off a handful of her clothes and flung them out, trying to burrow deeper into the closet, looking for some trace of her, looking for any part of my Karen that remained.

I ripped apart the closet looking for her, and then I started on the drawers, and the cupboards, and then the photographs in their frames, then the cardboard boxes of old crap in the garage. When I was done my fingers were bleeding, I don't know from what, and the house was trashed, and I was sitting in the hallway surrounded by everything Karen and I used to own together.

I sat there for a long time.

In the morning— I slept on the couch because I couldn't stand the thought of going to bed alone— I woke up knowing exactly what to do. Karen was still in Japan, so that was where I had to go. I wasn't being crazy, I understood that she was gone, but the part of her that I needed to say goodbye to, the part of her that I couldn't find around me, that was still in Japan.

I had spent very little money in the last year, just basic groceries, gas, the mortgage payment, and a six pack of beer every six days. I was actually surprised by how much money I had in my account. More than enough to book the flight for two days later and the room in the hotel that Karen and I had stayed at. The room she died in was occupied, but I got one across the hall and a promise from the receptionist that if it vacated while I was there I could move in to it.

I spent the next two days cleaning up everything I had wrecked. It was amazingly easy to throw out things that had once belonged to Karen, or that we had bought together. I thought I would be sentimental, when I started, but I wasn't. It was just stuff. It wasn't her.

The plane ride, including a couple stopovers, took almost two days. I was groggy and sweaty and oddly buzzing when I got to the hotel. Everything looked the same. It was eight in the morning, and people were just coming down for breakfast.

"Hi," I told the receptionist. "I'm checking in. My name is George Bennet."

"Oh, okay, let me have a look here…" the receptionist, a spritely young woman with short black hair clicked around at her computer, before looking up at me, disappointed. "I'm sorry sir, your room won't be ready until three."

"Oh," I said.

"Our complimentary hot breakfast is being served now, you could eat and if you like I can suggest some local attractions?"

'I might just hang around the lobby. When does the bar open?"

"Eleven."

"Okay, is there somewhere I can leave my bag?"

"Yes, of course, I'll just write up a tag for you here.... There you go, just hand that to whoever is behind the desk when you come back."

"Thanks."

I left my suitcase with her, and wandered off into the line of people waiting for breakfast. There was lots of stuff that looked good: bacon, eggs, French toast, but my stomach felt heavy from traveling. I ended up just taking a bowl of chopped up fruit and a coffee. I leafed through a newspaper while I ate, not really reading the words, just kind of letting it all wash past me apathetically.

After breakfast I roamed around the hotel, remembering

the pool that Karen and I swam in, the restaurant off the lounge, where we ate our first dinner in Japan, oh, and the stairwell where we snuck off for some quick, groping, frantic sex like we were teenagers again.

Eventually I settled into the hotel's business center to check emails and let my parents know I had landed safely. After that I started looking up deadly spiders. Would you believe that I had never bothered to find out what killed Karen? Poisonous giant spider had always been enough for me. Now that I was back in Japan, I found insatiable curiosity.

And immediate frustration. I started by just looking up deadliest local spiders, but I didn't find anything deadly enough, or large enough. The Joro spider had venom that was painful, but certainly not deadly, and it was named after some sort of mythological spider. And the little guy was yellow. I expanded my search to world's deadliest spiders, but the worst of the worst, the Sydney funnel-web spider, looked nothing like what had killed Karen. Also, it was Australian. All the others had low fatality rates, and also did not look like what killed Karen.

I dove right in, looking for anything, absolutely anything, that could explain what I saw that night. I learned a lot about arachnids, venom, and all sorts of gross shit, but nothing about spider the size of a human head with green eyes.

I became feverish. It was after lunch and I was very angry by the time I stopped. I stomped off to the lounge, and ordered a double scotch. I bolted the first drink and ordered another before the bartender had even put the bottle away. After the third drink I started to slow down on.

"I knew you'd be here."

It was a woman speaking behind me in a heavy yet elegant accent. I registered her perfectly fine, I just didn't realize she was talking to me. Even when she sat down on the barstool next to me, looking right at me, I kept my eyes on my drink.

"George, right?"

I looked up at her, brown hair, green eyes, sad smile, gentle Japanese features. She was beautiful. I wondered about the eyes. She was the only Japanese woman I had seen with brown hair and green eyes. Maybe she had some European in her family history.

"I'm sorry?"

"It's George, right?"

"Ah, yeah, yes, I'm sorry, have we met?"

"We have, a little over a year ago. I was one of the responding paramedics when... well, when we were called in to

293

your room."

"Oh."

"I knew you would be here. Don't ask me how I just knew."

"I couldn't find my wife back home."

"Well, no…"

"I mean, I couldn't say goodbye to her. I came back to say goodbye to her."

"Oh, of course, I didn't mean to be rude."

"It's okay. I'm sorry, I'm kind of a mess right now. It was a really long plane ride, and my room isn't ready until three, and I can't find the spider that killed Karen."

"It's five right now, love."

"Oh."

"What do you mean you couldn't find the spider?"

"Online. I don't know what kind of spider killed her. I can't find it. Do you know?"

The world was spinning. She looked so sad. I'm sure I seemed crazy but I didn't know how to explain that I hadn't felt a thing for a year and now I was feeling everything.

"Look, tell you what, let's get you into your room, I'll go retrieve your key with you, then you get a good sleep and tomorrow we can have dinner, alright?"

"Yes, okay."

She took me by the arm. Her fingers were very strong, I felt each one clenching around my bicep. I stood leaning against the counter, hearing words but not understanding them, while she had a short, animated conversation with a man behind a marble counter. Then her strong fingers again, down a rolling hall, into a jolting elevator. I was cold and sweating and awful. I tried to turn my face away, but she had me.

She took me to a room, where a man in red clothes was waiting with my suitcase. We both went in together, all three of us. I was put onto a bed and left in the dark, and the darkness found me and pulled me in. I dreamt of green eyes.

I woke up with urgency, understanding that my fever had broken. There was light coming in from the window. I rolled out of bed, where I had slept on top of the covers in my clothes, and fumbled for the bedside lamp until I found the switch and turned it on. The room was a carbon copy of the one I had shared with Karen, except in reverse. The flat screen TV was in the same spot in front of the king-size, the love seat was by the window still, and the writing desk was by the door. The bathroom was made up just the same, with the same brands of shampoo, and the towels folded into the same flower shapes.

I stood up, and got myself a bottle of water from the mini fridge. II probably cost fifteen dollars, but I downed it without a thought. My suitcase was standing by the door. I retrieved my shaving kit and a change of clothes, then went off to shower and clean up.

I felt better when I was finished, much better, and also much more confused. What the hell was I doing back in Japan? I had booked the trip in a frenzy, had arrived in a daze, and now that I was back and clear headed I thought maybe I had made a mistake.

Then I saw the note on the desk.

The name Jin, and a phone number. I had feverish flashes of sad green eyes and a grip so strong it hurt my arm. Pretty red lips with white teeth.

I thought for a while that I might not call her, as I went around unpacking my bag, placing items into the closet and the drawers beneath the TV. By the time I was done I was thinking about dinner, feeling very hungry, and I thought to myself Why would I eat alone when a beautiful young woman wants to eat with me? So I called her.

"George!" she exclaimed, as if we had been friends for years. "I was getting worried."

"I slept all day, and I only just finished getting set up."

"Great, great, are you hungry? You must be starving."

"That's actually why I was calling you. I thought I 'd take you up on your offer of dinner."

"Sure. Why don't we meet in the hotel lobby in fifteen minutes? Actually, better make it half an hour."

"Sure, see you then."

"See you then!"

I hung up the phone, and proceeded to waste time in front of the TV until it was time to meet Jin. I ended up in the lobby ten minutes early anyways, shaking a little. I don't know why I was nervous. It's not like it was a date. She was just someone who felt bad for me.

At least that's what I was telling myself, until She showed up in a thigh length, tight red dress. It was not the dress of a woman who felt bad for a man.

"Hello, George," said Jin, her brown hair falling in waves to her shoulders. I was suddenly very aware of the jeans and red and white checkered shirt I had tucked into them.

"You look like a picture."

"You're sweet."

"Did you have anywhere in mind? Am I underdressed?"

"You look very handsome, and everyone will excuse a Westerner," she said, taking my arm and leading me out of the lobby. Again, I noticed her strength. I don't think I could have beaten her if we arm wrestled. "Come on, the place is just up the street."

She took me to the restaurant that Karen and I had planned on going to for dinner the day she died. I didn't recognize it at first, but after ordering the appetizers it suddenly clicked, and I remembered why I was back.

"Do you know what killed Karen?" I asked suddenly, breaking off our conversation about shrimp versus prawns. "I can't find the kind of spider I saw anywhere."

"What kind of spider do you think you saw?" All traces of mirth had slipped away from Jin's face. She adjusted the prawns on her plate.

"It was huge. As big as her head. With spiky brown hair and eight green eyes, and fangs the size of my fingers. I'll never forget that thing."

"I don't know any spiders like that. I thought the report said it was a centipede."

"No, I looked at dozens of pictures of them yesterday, there is no way that's what killed her."

"I don't know what to tell you George."

"Yeah. Okay."

Dinner interrupted the uncomfortable silence that followed. I had fish, she had a rare steak. We started talking and joking again soon after, and ordered another bottle of red wine. We spoke of other things.

I'm not sure how it happened. I know I can't take credit for it. Jin walked me back to my room, her fingers again around my arm. Then we were just kissing, not even bothering turning the lights on, clothes were falling off us as if on their own. We made love, sad, desperate, clinging love, the kind to broken people use to remind themselves that life is bigger than their problems. It was beautiful, in the sort of way that I didn't really believe it was happening until it was over. I didn't have a condom, but she told me it wasn't a problem, and I believed her.

When it was over, I wished that it wasn't. Jin reached into her purse and pulled out an eye mask.

"Will you wear this for me, please? I have a phobia. I hate when people watch me sleep."

"Oh, um, okay, sure."

"Promise me you'll keep it on all night?"

"Yeah, I promise."

I put the black mask over my eyes, and naked, we fell asleep within seconds. I think she got up for a while, and opened a window. I'm not sure, I just remember waking up once and she wasn't in my arms any more, and I had this breezy sensation all over my body. When I woke up she was there again.

The week that followed was like a dream. One by one, without ever discussing it, Jin took me to every single place that Karen had wanted to go. Either Karen and I were the most clichéd tourist's possible, or I had a type. Sometimes, in a dizzy whirl of suspicion, I wondered if somehow, someway, Jin knew. Like she had claimed to know that I would be back at the hotel on the very day that I returned, or maybe she had stolen Karen's journal when she responded. I didn't know, and the moments of doubt grew fewer the more time I spent with Jin. We saw a museum all about the Samurai, and the cherry blossom festival which Karen's and my whole trip had been planned around. We ate just so much mazing sushi. Every night, we would get back to the room and fuck like we were in a romance novel. It was amazing, every time, and then she would pull out her night mask and ask me to put it on, every time explaining that she had a phobia, she couldn't stand people watching her sleep.

This was funny because I don't think that she actually slept that much. More and more in the night, I would wake up and feel nobody beside me, but feel a breeze, or the covers pulling against me, or maybe just the loss of her warmth against me, either way it was like something running all the way over me. I would have been bothered more by it, but I knew my return trip was coming up. I had booked two weeks in Japan, and time was running out. I think we both knew that, so I didn't let myself get too curious about what Jin did at night. We were just having fun, and whatever her trauma was, the less I knew the better.

Until two days before I left.

We were sitting in a bar, having sake, Jin as usual looked spectacular in a blue floral dress. Her eyes were sadder than usual. She touched my hand.

"I can't stand the thought of you going."

"I know, it has been a great two weeks, better than I could have imagined, but I can't stay here forever."

"I know, but I could go with you."

"For a how long? Don't you have to go back to work at

some point?"

"Well, if we were married…"

"Married?"

"Why not? I love you George. I don't want this to end, ever."

"Well, there's just so much we don't know about each other…"

"But I want to know it about you, George," she took my hand, leaning in, her big green eyes wide, her fingers holding me firmly. I felt a tiny little prick on the palm of my hand, probably from her ring, but I felt a tingle spreading from it. "Please, I know it sounds crazy, but I promise we will make it work. I will make you so happy George."

The list of reasons I had not to marry her melted away, as she leaned closer, held me harder.

"Okay."

"Yes?"

"Yes."

"Yes!" cried Jin, and for the first time, her eyes were not sad.

I lay awake that night, eyes open beneath the sleep mask.

All the questions that I had put out of my mind about Jin were suddenly rattling around, louder than anything thing else.

How did she know? Everything she knew, that I came back to Japan, all the places Karen and I had wanted to go. And why couldn't I look at her when she was sleeping?

That one was easy to solve, at least. Ever so cautiously, as if I were just moving a little in my sleep, I slid my face down the pillow a little, so that the mask was displaced over my right eye. The room was dark, lit only a little by the digital clock on the microwave, the alarm clock on Jin's side of the bed, and a trickle of light slipping in beneath the door and one edge of the window where the blinds weren't all the way shut. I could make out shapes, no colors.

Jin's body was there, on her back, perfectly normal. Maybe she really did just have some weird thing.

Which kind of put things in perspective; I was obsessing over little, perfectly explainable things because I had only known Jin for two weeks. I was nervous about marrying a woman I had only just met, but need I be? We we're so connected.

That's what I was thinking about when the digital clock turned to midnight, and Jin burst apart.

Her body just disintegrated, scattering across the room,

running in every direction, all over me towards the window, the door, anywhere. I felt a sensation like a breeze as whatever it was skittered across me.

One of them went right over my face, right over my exposed eye. Eight legs, a bulbous yellow abdomen, two fangs glinting. Then it was gone.

I sat up, tore the mask off my space. Dozens of spiders scattered off my body.

"What the fuck!" I screamed, and then I saw it, and then it saw me.

Eight emerald green eyes turned to me, on the pillow next to me. Bristling brown hair. A spider the size of a human head.

"George, go back to sleep," said the spider in Jin's voice. "You are dreaming. It's only a dream."

"What are you?" I cried, reaching for something, anything. My hand grabbed the heavy bedside lamp. "What the fuck are you!"

"I am Jorōgumo," said Jin, stepping towards me on it's eight long legs. "Please, George, put the lamp down. I love you. I only want to be with you."

"You killed Karen! You killed my wife!"

I swung the lamp, down, onto the pillow where the spider stood, but all I hit was the pillow. The lightbulb shattered anyway. Jin leapt, her eight legs stabbing into my chest as she latched on.

"This is the only way my love."

And her fangs stabbed into my heart.

I don't know where I am now. I cannot move. There are thick cords of silken web all around me, and it is dark most of the time. Once in a while, through the pulling of the webs, I feel movement. I picture Karen, trapped here, paralyzed by the same venom that paralyzed me, her body swapped out by the paramedic posing as a human. I wondered whose ashes were on my bookshelf. I wondered whose ashes would be sent back to my parents. I call out, but no one ever answers. Until she comes back. Every night, she comes back. Always hungry for the same meal… me. She tells me she loves me as her spider's body takes me. She tells me our children are beautiful.

And I am trapped, the husband of Jorōgumo, unable to do anything but recall my own foolishness, and how it led me here. And beg, I can still do that.

Acknowledgements

Dragon's Roost Press would like to extend its sincerest gratitude to a number of people.

First and foremost, we would like to thank the authors whose works fill these pages. Thank you for taking us to strange places and introducing us to a wild menagerie of cryptids. Your new take on familiar – and some not so familiar – beasts is truly inspiring.

The editing staff would also like to thank all of the authors who submitted during our open call, but whose stories were not selected. Even after extending the project to two volumes, we still had stories which we loved but simply did not have room for. We wish the best to you all.

Enormous thanks to all of our Kickstarter supporters: fill in the names here. This was our first time running an "all or nothing" campaign and we were more than a little worried. Without your support, these books simply would not exist.

Thank you to Luke Spooner whose art graces our covers. You captured the look we were aiming for exactly. We are sure that everyone is tired of us whipping out our phones to show them the beautiful covers.

We tip our glasses to the members of the Great Lakes Association of Horror Writers, the attendees of AthanorCon, and all of our friends in the writing and horror communities. You inspire us.

Acknowledgements

Thank you to all of the friends and supporter of Dragon's Roost Press who follow us on the blog, on social media, and who visit us at our convention appearances, as well as all of our readers (including you, yes you, holding the book right now!). You are the reason that we do what we do.

Thank you to our Kickstarter Backers: Asher, Rose M Anderson, Josh Bowen, Lat Brown, Andy Busch, Nicole Castle-Kelly, Anton Cancre, Dan Chisholm, Aleta Clegg, Crispymayhem, the DeVito family, Sarah Doebereiner, R Fletcher, Peter Guenther, Ivan, Jen Haeger, Josh Hendren, Stephen Hunt, jrho, jmrozanski, Jonna, Justin, Connie Lagge, James Lucas, Alexander Lyle, Kurtis Primm, William Robertson, Tori Smith, Edward Stasheff , Liz T, Alana Thibert, Rebecca Try, Cindy Williams, Andrew Wright, and those who wished to remain annonymous.

Long walks and warm snuggle to assistant editors Tesla and Titus. Thank you for putting up with long hours and the computer and for making us take breaks when we needed them.

Finally, all of my love and appreciation to Ruth Pinto-Cieslak who puts up with a ridiculous amount of nonsense with a smile and a nod. There is no one I would rather go hunting mysterious creatures with.

About the Contributors

Jaleta Clegg ("Finding a Purpose")loves to play, "What if?" She loves good fight scenes, adventures, and explosions, so her stories tend to feature these elements. She writes space opera, science fiction adventure, fantasy of all flavors, and silly horror. When not writing, she enjoys watching bad monster movies and 80s sci-fi shows, sharing strange music videos from YouTube with her kids (it's a contest to see who can find the worst), and crocheting monsters. Cthulhu toilet paper cozies, anyone?

A. Collingwood's ("Spider") previously published work includes the stories "Angus" in *Morpheus Tales*, "Daylight" in *Bloodbond* magazine, "Miskatonic University" in the anthology *Miskatonic Nightmares*, and "Family Dinner" in the anthology *The Year's Best Body Horror*.

Sarah Doebereiner ("Hellhound") is an author, editor, and avid reader from central Ohio. She graduated from Wright State University in 2010 with her BA in English. Macabre themes fascinate her because of their tendency to stay with readers long after the book closes. Sarah currently works for Claren Books as their Acquisitions / General Editor. Connect with her via Facebook at https://www.facebook.com/sarahadoebereiner.

JG Faherty ("Devils in the Dark") is a Thriller Award and multiple Bram Stoker Award nominee and an Active Member of the HWA, SFWA, MWA, RWA, and ITW. His credits include 5 novels, 9 novellas, and more than 50 short stories in professional markets.

Zachary Finn ("The Invisible Beast") was born and raised in Rochester, NY. He studied history at Lycoming College (BA) and SUNY Brockport (MA), and currently he lives with his two pit bull mixes, Bruce and Buster. In his free time, he enjoys training Brazilian jiu-jitsu, and coaching wrestling.

Erik Goldsmith ("From the Second Mouth")is a high school English teacher in Houston where he lives with his wife and son. He is an avid reader and has a book of short stories coming out in November from Scarlet Leaf Publishing house.

Sarah Hans ("Iceheart") is an award-winning writer, editor, and teacher. Sarah's short stories have appeared in over twenty publications, but she's best known for her multicultural steampunk anthology *Steampunk World*. You can read more of her short stories, nonfiction ramblings, and novel chapters on her Patreon for just $1/month at https://www.patreon.com/sarahhans or find her on twitter at https://twitter.com/steampunkpanda.

"Not content to conquer the rock music world, Matt Hayward ("An Unusual Pet")has now turned his attention to dark fiction, and how much richer we all are as a result. *Brain Dead Blues* is everything you'd expect from a rock star turned horror writer, documenting not only facets of the music world but also the darkness that can result from obsessions both creative and violent. I have long been a fan of both the music and the man behind it. Now I'm a fan of his writing too." - Kealan Patrick Burke, Bram Stoker Award-winning author of *The Turtle Boy*, *Kin*, and *Sour Candy*.

Adam Millard ("Picnicking with Old Yellow Top") is the author of twenty-six novels, twelve novellas, and more than two hundred short stories, which can be found in various collections, magazines, and anthologies. Probably best known for his post-apocalyptic and comedy-horror fiction, Adam also writes fantasy/horror for children, as well as bizarro fiction for several publishers. His work has recently been translated for the German market.

Frances Pauli ("Please Don't Feed the Howler") is the hybrid author of over twenty novels and numerous short stories. Her work has appeared in *Daily Science Fiction*, *Flash Fiction Online*, *Silver Blade*, and the *Shanghai Steam* and *Strange Little Girls* anthologies. She lives in Washington State and keeps a variety of unusual pets, but so far, no cryptids.

One of Michael Penncavage's ("The Corn Bear")stories, "The Cost of Doing Business," recently published in *Thuglit*, won the Derringer Award for Best Short Mystery. Another one of his stories, "The Converts" was recently adapted into a short film.

His fiction can be found in approximately 90 magazines and anthologies from many different countries such as *Alfred Hitchcock Mystery Magazine*, *Here and Now*, *Crime Factory*, *Tenebres*, *Reaktor*, *Visionarium*, and *Speculative Mystery*.

Lauren E Reynolds ("A Day in the Life of Cactus Cat") has been writing since she was eight years old, and decided, rather boldly, that she would become a Writer as an adult. Since then she has graduated from the State University of New York Oneonta with a Bachelors of Science in English with a duel minor in History and Creative Writing, and has written hundreds of poems and short stories, which she is putting into a collection, and several novels she hopes to publish in the near future. Her dream is to one day write and publish a series. She currently lives in Bel Air Maryland with her family and works as a freelance Writer, artist and Librarian. When she is not writing she enjoys going for walks with her dog, researching, and taking long hikes in the woods looking for animals, both known and not yet identified.

Samantha Rich ("Many Rivers") lives in the DC suburbs with a (grumpy) cat and a (nervous) dog. She is a lifelong fan of speculative fiction.

Joette Rozanski ("Holiday Hunt") is a native of Toledo, Ohio, where she works as a free-lance desktop publisher. She enjoys photography as much as writing, which includes science fiction, fantasy, horror and humor. Joette's had stories published in the anthologies *Sword and Sorceress XIII, Such a Pretty Face, Nights of Blood II, Strangely Funny*, and *Tomorrow's Cthulhu*. Her novel, *The Search for a Sipping House*, is an e-book about a very different sort of vampire.

Lynn Rushlau ("An Exchange of Fear") graduated from the University of Texas with a degree in Anthropology and minor in Sociology--which seem like awesome planning for a life creating cultures and societies, but she'll admit to not have been thinking that far in advance. She lives in Addison, Texas with two attention-needy cats, and can be found on twitter at lrushlau.

Paul Stansfield ("The Keystone State") was born and raised in New Jersey, and works as a field archaeologist. He has had over 20 short stories published in magazines, including *Bibliophilos, Morbid Curiosity, Cthulhu Sex Magazine, In D'tale*, and *The Literary Hatchet*. He currently has stories in 6 horror anthologies, including *Cranial Leakage Vol. 2* (Grinning Skull Press), and *Creepy Campfire Quarterly Vol. 1* and *The Prison Compendium*, both from EMP Publishing. He is an Affiliate Member of the Horror Writers Association. His personal blog address is: http://paulstansfield.blogspot.com

Dale Sproule ("Two Yurts") is a writer, editor and reviewer. His fiction has appeared in *Northern Frights, Tesseracts, Pulphouse, Ellery Queen's Mystery Magazine, Pseudopod, The Colored Lens*, and about 40 others. He has been nominated for the Aurora Award 8 times and 17 of his stories were collected in *Psychedelia Gothique*.

In the 90s, he co-published and edited (with Sally McBride) a magazine called *Trans Versions – Literature of the Fantastic*. He's just putting the finishing touches on a big muti-genre novel called *Avenging Glory*.

Nemma Wollenfang ("Spring-heeled Jack: The Terror of London") is an MSc Postgraduate of Vector Biology and Parasitology whose stories have appeared in three of Flame Tree's bestselling Gothic Fantasy hardbacks: *Science Fiction Short Stories, Murder Mayhem,* and *Pirates & Ghosts*, among other publications. One of her unpublished novels won the Retreat West First Chapter Competition as well as gaining Honorable Mentions for the SLF's Working Class Writers' Grant in 2015 and 2016. She has also gained a Silver Honorable Mention in Writers of the Future, been Highly Commended in the Stratford-Upon-Avon Short Story Competition, and won first place in the Northwich LitFest Short Story Competition. She can be found on Facebook and Twitter: @NemmaW.

About Last Day Dog Rescue

Last Day is more than just a name, it's the situation all the dogs were faced with. Because of LDDR these wonderful dogs get another chance at life. All dogs coming into their rescue were saved from high-kill animal shelters or being sold for research.

A Little About LDDR:

Last Day Dog Rescue is an ALL volunteer based organization. They do not have a physical location; all of their dogs are placed in the care of foster homes until they are adopted.

The group focuses on rescuing dogs from the "Urgent" list in shelters and pounds across lower Michigan and parts of Ohio with an emphasis on those shelters who euthanize by gas or those shelters who sell the dogs in their care to research labs where they are used for barbaric and most times painful testing and experiments. They hold a special place in their hearts for the big and black dogs, even 'ugly' dogs (whom they don't find ugly at all!) and the special senior dogs. These dogs most often get overlooked and passed up in shelters and pounds everywhere for puppies, small breeds, and the "prettier," lighter colored dogs.

Dogs found in shelters are there for many reasons; some are owner surrenders, strays, cruelty or abuse cases, and some dogs are found abandoned, left to fend for themselves in vacant homes, fields, ditches, and some have even been tied out in the woods and left to starve. Last Day Dog Rescue does not discriminate and feels that each of these dogs, no matter their size, age, color, or the reason they are there, deserve a second chance at life...they help all those they can.

Donations via check and money orders:
Last Day Dog Rescue
P.O. Box 51935
Livonia, MI 48151-5935

Donations also accepted via PayPal:
http://www.lastdaydogrescue.org/info/

Dragon's Roost Press is the fever dream brainchild of dark speculative fiction author Michael Cieslak. Since 2014, their goal has been to find the best speculative fiction authors and share their work with the public. For more information about Dragon's Roost Press and their publications, please visit: http://thedragonsroost.net/styled-3/index.html.

A portion of the proceeds from all sales of *Hidden Menagerie Vol 1* will be donated to the Last Day Dog Rescue Organization.

Be sure to check out the companion volume *Hidden Menagerie Vol 2*

Edited by Michael Cieslak

Also Available from Dragon's Roost Press

Robotic Animals
Televisions Which Reveal Alternate Universes
Inanimate Objects Brought to Life
People Struggling to Survive in Apocalyptic Wastelands
Sentient Cutlery

and much, much more

Desolation: 21 Tales for Tails is a collection of dark speculative fiction whose stories all focus on themes of loneliness, isolation, and abandonment.

Enter into strange worlds envisioned by some of the most inventive writing today.

Combine the mind splintering horror of the Cthulhu Mythos and the heart shattering portion of that most terrible of emotions -- love -- and what do you have? You have *Eldritch Embraces: Putting the Love Back in Lovecraft*.

This collection of short stories from some of the best authors working in the fields of horror and dark speculative fiction blends romance and Lovecraft in a way which will make you sigh, smile, weep, or leave you the hollow shell of your former self.

A portion of the proceeds of each sale of *Desolation: 21 Tales for Tails* and *Eldritch Embraces: Putting the Love Back in Lovecraft* benefit the Last Day Dog Rescue Organization.

Also Available from Dragon's Roost Press

The Maiden's Courage

by Mary Lynne Gibbs

The best man on the pirate ship is a girl named Alex.

Alexandra "Alex" Gardner is the reluctant cabin boy on *The Bloody Maiden*, a ruthless pirate ship run by the charmingly evil Captain Montgomery. The crew is convinced she's a boy, and she hopes it stays that way until she has the chance to avenge the deaths of her mother and brother at the hands of the crew. All goes well until the ship takes a handsome captive. Could her feelings for him ruin her charade?

Sebastian Whitley is a young man in love. He sails on his father's ship, trying to find the beautiful girl he's lost. When he's captured by *The Bloody Maiden*, the annoying cabin boy saves his life – and makes it more difficult at the same time. His savior is actually a girl, and if Sebastian doesn't keep quiet, it could mean both their deaths. Together, they have to thwart a mutiny, get revenge, and get off the ship before Alex's secret is revealed. If not, it's the plank for both of them.

Also Available from Dragon's Roost Press

Jericho Rising

by Mary Lynne Gibbs

In post-World War III, small town Michigan, a self-proclaimed, violent, and insane High Priestess has taken control, reducing the remaining men to nothing more than slaves and playthings. Jericho, the reluctant leader of the Resistance, must fight her own family to preserve the freedom and equality of all in her care – male and female alike. She's torn between love and duty, and with traitors around every corner, she has no idea who to trust anymore.

Jericho's Redemption

by Mary Lynne Gibbs

The battle is over, but the war has just begun. Jericho returns to the Obsidian camp, only to learn that her sister Candace destroyed it as part of a plot to dismantle the resistance movement that brought down their mother, the High Priestess. The rest of the resistance blames Jericho for the deaths of their friends, but that's the least of her worries. Not only does Jericho now have to right the wrongs her sister has done, she must contend with a few guests to the camp who bring secrets that will change her life forever. Either she'll redeem herself in the eyes of her comrades, or she'll die t rying.

Also Available from Dragon's Roost Press

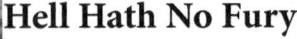

Hell Hath No Fury

by Peggy Christie

Ever wonder how you might handle a sabbatical from work? Think the bible told you everything there is to know about the Devil? What if the noises coming from under your child's bed weren't just in his imagination? Crack open *Hell Hath No Fury*, a collection of 21 tales of horror and dark fiction, to learn the answers to these questions. Discover stories of psychotic delusions, ghosts, a murder victim's revenge, and a family brought closer together through torture.

Sex, Gore, and Millipedes

by Ken MacGregor

Ken MacGregor, known for pushing boundaries in horror, for shoving the reader outside of their comfort zone, has finally gone too far. *Sex, Gore, and Millipedes* is a collection of the sickest stuff you've ever read. This book will hit your triggers. Hopefully, all of them. You've been warned.